Teagan's Treasure

Emerald Isle University Series

Book #1

COLLEEN MARIE

Advance Praise for *Teagan's Treasure*

"Teagan's Treasure is a story that has what teen girls love - a strong and relatable female main character in a story that is filled with romance, mystery, and horses! It also has what moms want - a quality story line for their daughters that is wholesome and pure. As a mom of 5 daughters, I am grateful for authors like Colleen Marie." ~ Kelly Ann Guest, author of *Saintly Moms: 25 Stories of Holiness* and mother of 9

"Teagan's Treasure is an engaging story about finding your path in life. I truly enjoyed the wholesome yet intriguing story that included just the right balance of mystery, danger, risk taking, treasure hunting, and young love." ~ Mary Jo Puglisi, MS, Licensed Clinical Professional Counselor (LCPC)

"Teagan's Treasure will take you on a family-friendly adventure along the Irish countryside, filled with treasure hunting, mystery, academic pursuits, choosing life paths and young love. The characters are relatable, strong and driven and the storyline is completely captivating. Colleen Marie writes beautifully and vividly with positive and wholesome messaging about faith, hope and following your dreams. This engaging and heartfelt novel is a must read for young adult readers!" ~ Tiffany Noone, Writer, Homesteader & Homeschool Mom at Fern Woods Farm

"Colleen Marie weaves a captivating and compassionate tale of young love and Irish adventure in Teagan's Treasure, the first installment in the Emerald Isle's series. A true servant's heart is displayed in Teagan, the curious and kind protagonist, as she pursues her dreams of helping others find healing and confidence through equine therapy with the help of a lovable cast of characters. Teagan's Treasure has the perfect dose of intrigue and mystery to balance out the homey and humorous undertones of the story. I eagerly await the next installment." ~ Allison Ramirez, author of The Divided Kingdom series

"As Teagan immerses herself in the Irish culture during a summer University research program, she discovers sweet and complicated young love, an adventure-filled hunt for treasure, and the unique bond between horses and humans. This family-friendly young adult novel, which are often hard to come by, fills a much-needed gap in literature by appropriately exploring healthy relationships of all kinds, growing in faith as a young adult, pursuing academic passions and friends becoming family. Anyone who loves horses will especially enjoy learning as they read about Teagan and Finn's research on equine-assisted activities, with children with disabilities, that take place at a beautiful, old, family farm in the Irish countryside. You will feel like you are in Ireland yourself as the characters speak their unique Irish English, pass on their captivating family stories, eat traditional Irish meals, and visit Dublin and the green rolling hills of the countryside." ~ Christen Purcell, M.Ed. School Counseling

To Connor, Brody, and Emma Rose—
May you always find your treasure.

Prologue

High School - Freshman Year

A silver paper clip sailed across the classroom and collided with a model frog skeleton on the windowsill. The tiny foot snapped like a parched twig and tumbled to the hard, linoleum floor. A cheer erupted from the jocks in the back of the room, muffling my sigh.

"Bullseye!" Scott Anderson boomed, fist-punching the air. His buddies cheered him on like he had just won the Nobel prize for discovering a cure for cancer. Wait…who am I kidding? They cheered as if he'd caught the winning touchdown pass in the town's annual Turkey Bowl, an accomplishment that definitely would make the headlines around here.

Seriously, how did they find those games funny year after year? Freshman year hadn't been the change I hoped to see. For that matter, high school itself wasn't quite the experience I'd imagined.

I snapped the little frog-foot back in place, then let out a frustrated groan as the chipped bones swayed a bit to the side.

Scott sent me a beaming smile, quirking his head the same way he had when we'd played together as kids. He was always the one for mischief, while I'd been left to bail him out. Despite my blatant eye roll, he headed my way, hopping over a few desks in the process.

He propped himself on the empty one beside me. "Hey, Teagan. How's it going?"

"Fine." I shook my head to loosen his gentle tug on my ponytail—another thing that hadn't changed since childhood.

"So, who's taking you to the Spring Fling?"

Couldn't anyone talk about anything else? No one around here saw anything outside of our small town and its outdated traditions. "I'm not sure I'm even going."

"You gotta go. Come with me. It'll be fun." His eyes took on that mischievous glint that always came before what was certain to be a fun-but-foolish adventure.

Jamie gasped behind me, and I almost laughed out loud. An invitation from Scott to…well, anywhere…would probably be a dream for most girls in our class. For me, though, the guy was like a brother—a loud, annoying, rowdy one. Granted, he was also cute and lovable in his own way, but still a huge pain.

So, while going to the dance with Scott wasn't a dream come true for me, it was better than being set up by one of my friends and having to make tedious conversation all night with some guy I didn't even know. If I was going to get dragged to the dance anyway, I might as well go with him.

I shrugged. "Sure, why not?"

"Ah, the answer every guy wants to hear." He laughed and tugged my ponytail one last time before heading back to his buddies. "I'll call you."

I nodded without looking back.

Jamie sighed. "You're so lucky."

Before I could respond, the classroom door swung open.

"Attention, class!" Mrs. Benson hollered the greeting as she spun on one heel. "We have a very special guest today." She swung one arm in a lavish flourish as a man followed her into the room. "This is Mr. Sean Fitzpatrick, program director of the Emerald Isle University's Science Research Scholar's Program."

Wearing green plaid pants, a brown sweater vest, and swinging a walking stick, Mr. Fitzpatrick might have stepped straight out of an Irish fairytale. To further the illusion, a black tweed cap sat slightly askew on his round head, and wiry red hair poked out from under the brim.

As the funny-looking man talked about the research program, I sat up straighter and leaned forward, the tingle of a new dream taking root. The possibility of an adventure—one Scott's antics could never come close to matching—called to me from somewhere in the distance. All thoughts of the Spring Fling disappeared from my mind. I envisioned instead the possibility of a very different future—one where I'm far, far away in a land of rolling green hills and magical tales.

And so my story begins.

Chapter One

Three Years Later

Certain moments in life change everything, and nothing will ever be the same again. Moments when, in an instant, past years drift away in a swirl of memories, like a fractured prelude to the life you were meant to live. Those moments come like a whisper but the story shouts for an eternity.

My moment comes one Saturday morning, a month before my high school graduation. I swallow a scream as I examine the well-worn and -traveled package in the mailbox. The antique Dublin postmark in the upper right corner confirms my hopes that the package holds the answer to an unspoken prayer deep in my heart, one I've held tightly for the past three years.

My heart races as I carry the package to my bedroom and quickly close the door behind me. Laying it on my bed with the same care I might give a priceless gem, I delicately loosen each strip of tape. Lifting the lid, I find a business envelope perched triumphantly on top of a collection of items wrapped in brown paper and held together with the embossed Emerald Isle University sticker…proof not only that I've been accepted, but that everything is about to change.

Last fall when I applied for the Emerald Isle Science Research Internship, a prestigious program for graduating seniors pursuing a career in the life sciences, I'd cast my net far and wide in hopes of catching a golden, faraway dream—a dream that included studying at Emerald Isle University in Dublin, Ireland. Students lucky enough to be selected for the summer program will get a chance to go to Ireland and compete for a spot in their coveted science research program. The team that comes up with the best research proposal will not only be awarded spots in the program, but will also receive a grant to fund their independent research with a mentor. My dream is to be one of those students, a dream that began three years earlier as I listened to Mr. Fitzpatrick talk about Emerald Isle University during freshman biology, and everything else faded away in comparison.

Mr. Fitzpatrick's presentation wasn't the first time I'd heard of Emerald Isle though. My parents attended Emerald Isle together, and as they'd said so many times over the years, it forever changed their lives. It's where their fairytale began and I hope mine will too.

~

Four weeks later, sunlight sends green sparkles dancing around the room as I clip my gold and emerald claddagh necklace, a graduation gift from my parents. Emeralds have a special meaning for me, not just because they're my birthstone, but because I feel connected to them in an inexplicable way. The stone represents loyalty, friendship, and faithfulness, which are values I've always held close to my heart. I also love that it's a youthful stone, green and hopeful. As I rub the smooth surface, all the hopes I've been holding inside begin to release and spring to life.

The airline ticket and summer itinerary on my desk serve as reminders that this was actually happening. No longer a distant dream, it's a reality that begins today. I will spend the next eight weeks in Ireland. I slip the ticket and program packet into my leather tote and secure the lock. I fold my white cardigan sweater and place it neatly inside before snapping the gold buckle, well aware of how chilly flights can get.

Laughter drifts up the stairs, filling my room with the sounds of home. The farewell lunch my parents planned is already underway. Walking out of my bedroom is like stepping into the future—a contrast to the actual steps, which are more reminiscent of the past with each creaking groan. We live in an 1800s-style farmhouse in northern Maryland, which is like being back in time, but with modern enhancements of electricity, running water, and indoor bathrooms. I stop on the landing and glance out the window at the horses grazing in the pasture. Turning, I run my fingers over the framed article from Equine Veterinary Medicine featuring my parents smiling brightly, our farmhouse standing strong in the background.

My parents bought this house just before they married, twenty-five years ago, and remodeled it room by room. They'd met while students studying abroad at Emerald Isle University in a grant-based program with Roisin University for Veterinary Medicine. They spent the first four years in Dublin and then the next four years in Ithaca, New York. They not only fell in love with equine medicine but with each other, dreaming of one day opening their own practice and raising a family in the country.

After graduating with DVMs and receiving job offers in California and Tennessee, my parents spent the next few years traveling across the country to see each other. The distance never decreased their love or dream for the future. When the time was right, they left their positions with excellent references and much-needed experience and invested in our 100-acre farm. They married one week after settling on the farm, at the local town chapel of Berryville. Afterward, they celebrated with family and friends at the farm, while feasting on steamed crabs and sweet corn.

They started O'Reilly Equine Veterinary shortly after, and never looked back. My parents are pretty much famous around here as a dynamic duo of vets. I wish I had known them when they first met, but seeing them together has always inspired me to find that kind of love and make my own dreams come true.

My sister, Kayleigh, approaches with a sullen expression. "What are we going to do?" she asks, wiping a tear from her cheek.

Kayleigh's always been the most dramatic of the three of us. And definitely the biggest hugger. She's only a year younger than me, and even at seventeen she has an innocence that makes her seem years younger. Her eyes, the same sky blue as mine, brim with tears. People sometimes confuse us for twins, and I can see why. At five foot six, with the same fair skin and long, dark hair, we look as close to twins as you can get.

"I'm gonna miss you so much!" Kayleigh wraps me in the biggest bear hug.

"Me too. But it's only for the summer," I remind her.

"Unless you win, which of course you will, and then you'll be in Ireland for years."

"She's leaving for two months, not two decades." Our youngest sister, Ashling, rolls her eyes as she walks by. "I'll miss you too, Teag, but can we at least get some food before the blubbering begins?"

Sixteen-year-old Ashling, with her shiny auburn hair and bright green eyes, acts like she's thirty-four with her worldly exasperation for all things overly emotional or dramatic, which basically means that she and Kayleigh rarely see eye to eye. Luckily, Kayleigh is so good-natured that she only sees the best in everyone, looking past Ashling's pointed remarks.

As much as Kayleigh and I look alike, Ashling looks like the odd one out—something I believe she takes to heart. While she has the same fair skin as us, her green eyes always appear to sparkle with a secret.

My stomach grumbles, reminding me that even though Ashling's just pushing Kayleigh's buttons, she does have a point. I gently pull Kayleigh along to our large wrap-around porch, the scent of grilling burgers and hotdogs wafting through the air. At least fifty people are gathered in the yard, and even more mill around the stables and land.

Mom is talking by the outdoor arena with Mrs. Miller as little Abby kisses Wilbur, our chestnut gelding, on the nose. Born with cerebral palsy, Abby has grown so much the past few months and mom believes she will begin to walk stronger soon. No doubt they will stay for the party too. Our farm is home to many in our small town.

The land, home to horses, goats, sheep, donkeys, chickens, and one spirited potbelly pig, is a sanctuary to many. The Claddagh Farm and Animal Rescue sign hangs at the entrance, its boldly carved letters contrasting with the natural wood, reminding everyone that this is a place of refuge for the unwanted and downtrodden. A new beginning. What started as a run-down farmhouse and overgrown land is now one of the most beautiful and welcoming farms in all of Maryland.

A green claddagh is painted in the center of the sign—two hands holding a heart with a crown on top, and symbolizing the place where my parents fell in love—a place I will be in less than twenty-four hours. *Friendship, Loyalty, and Love* is carved below the name, and I've never known a motto to be more appropriate. I join my family and friends, knowing I'm about to leave a very special home.

"Okay, enough of the tears already. Open mine," Ashling says with a teasing smile.

I laugh at the superhero wrapping paper, one of our shared loves.

"Are you sure it's safe to open?" I ask hesitantly. I can only imagine what Ashling has in this box. It could be anything from a book on how to snag a cute Irish guy to a living, breathing frog.

Ashling rolls her eyes. "Come on, Teag. You know me."

"Yeah, that's kinda the problem."

Laughter sounds around us as Ashling narrows her eyes, giving a playful flip of her hair.

I slowly open the box, fully on alert to catch something if it jumps out.

"Crabby Spice!" I exclaim, holding up one of the tiny packets of seafood seasoning.

"Oh, yeah," Dad cheers. "You won't find that over in Ireland."

I remove four travel-size packs of spices, a staple in our family. We've been putting Crabby Spice on everything for as long as I can remember. We often joke that our family could solely keep the company running.

Ashling looks pleased with herself. "We can't have you going all crazy over there when you order fries, or should I say 'chips,' and they don't have Crabby Spice. I mean, can you imagine?"

"Teagan without Crabby Spice? Nope, can't imagine that," Scott says.

"Come on, I'm not that predictable!" I push Scott's shoulder. Over the years, our friendship has grown despite our failed attempt at a romantic relationship. I find myself thankful for our shared history, and the way we were able to transition back to friends.

"Ah, yeah, you are. I bet if I opened your bag, you would have an old lady cardigan folded in a perfect square, arms at right angles, waiting right on top in case of an emergency on the plane, like a threatening breeze or worse—air conditioning."

"Well…that's only good sense," I grumble among the murmur of laughter and head nods. How everyone seems to think they know me is as annoying as it is comforting. *Could I really be that predictable?*

I'm about to put the containers back in the box when I notice something under the last of the tissue paper. Pulling out the rest of the paper reveals an eight-by-ten canvas painting at the bottom of the box.

"Oh, Assateague Island!" I hold the canvas closer to examine the paint strokes. "That was the best day!"

I gaze at the painting of the three of us sitting side by side on the beach at sunrise, gazing out to the ocean while the native horses cool off by the ocean.

Assateague Island, a small barrier island off the east coast of Maryland, is a favorite vacation spot for us. Herds of feral horses live there and some of my favorite memories are camping on the island with my sisters. We have always enjoyed our time together. Ashling painted us from the back. Our heads are turned toward each other, me laughing carefree and utterly happy. Kayleigh's warmth radiates in her smile, while Ashling's mouth is open as if in the middle of a joke. It's perfect—she captured us. And that's Ashling. A joke one moment, then touching your heart the next.

Reliving the memory may have been too much for Kayleigh though. She is quivering with emotion. Chris, her boyfriend, wraps a supportive arm around her shoulders. I catch Ashling rolling her eyes at them, and I wonder for the hundredth time how my sisters are going to survive the summer together.

"You know how much I'm going to miss you." Kayleigh's lips tremble and she pauses to still them. "I know we won't be able to talk every day, so I want you to have this." She barely gets out the last word before handing me a small box wrapped in delicate pink fabric and an olive-green bow.

The fabric falls away to reveal a brown leather journal. Neatly tucked into the front tie strap, a Micron 01 black pen awaits its first ink flow. After loosening the knot holding the journal shut, I open the cover to Kayleigh's neat handwriting on the first page.

Teagan,

It's the beginning of an unforgettable journey.
I hope you fill this journal with the most amazing memories!
xoxo
Kayleigh

The beginning of an unforgettable journey. I keep those words in mind as I say goodbye to everyone and leave with my parents for the airport. Even though we're leaving, the others will stay behind at the farm. They'll finish their food and conversations, then help with the clean-up before heading home themselves. Abby's eyes shine with wonder as she leans against her mom, fingers twisting the discarded ribbon from Kayleigh's gift to me. Our town is a family, one I can't imagine finding anywhere else.

~

The airport is bustling when we walk through the sliding doors.

"Watch it!" A man barks before barely missing us with a metal trolley loaded with suitcases. One bag hangs haphazardly to the side, threatening to escape its strap.

Dad's glasses slide down his nose. He shakes his head and looks at me with lips pursed. "Well, Teagan, this is as far as we can go."

"But we'll watch your plane take off," Mom promises.

She smiles up at Dad as he puts an arm around her shoulders. I'm sure this brings back memories from their own post-graduation flights to Ireland. Their experience at Emerald Isle University, meeting each other, falling in love, all leading to this life they've built. How many times have I heard them say that it was meant to be and how they may never have met each other if not for Ireland? I can't help but want to live that dream too.

"It's only eight weeks," I tell them. This has become a tagline for me recently.

A surreal feeling swirls around me as I watch my bags slide away on the conveyor belt with the bright yellow DUB tags. The next time I see them will be in Dublin Airport.

Dad checks his watch. "Right. But first, it's a seven-and-a-half-hour flight. Be sure to get some sleep."

"Enjoy every moment." As always, Mom balances Dad's practicality.

I return her smile and give her one last hug.

"And you are good with the currency transfer?"

"Yes, Dad. I have everything I need."

"Your jacket?"

"Dad! Yes, I have my jacket packed away." My blue all-weather rain jacket was a gift from my parents after being accepted into the program. "Always be prepared," Dad has always said, a true Boy Scout for life.

"Always be prepared for the rain." He points his finger towards the sky.

I suppress a laugh. "I know."

"Of course, she has her jacket, Patrick. I'm sure it's folded neatly in the bottom of her tote."

Seriously, am I really this predictable?

"It's actually on the side so—"

"So it'll be easier to get when you need it!" Mom taps her head with appreciation.

"Yeah," I murmur. "I should be prepared for anything."

I wave once more before entering the security check point. I've barely collected my carry-on bag when a woman's voice rings out.

"Teagan O'Reilly?"

A tall, slender woman in a sleek black suit and pale green blouse waves to me from a few feet away, her black high heels clicking. Long crimson curls bounce over her shoulders as her red lips part into a wide grin. Warm hazel eyes greet me as she extends a slender hand. "I'm Fiona Kelly, the US student ambassador for the Emerald Isle Scholars program. 'Tis so nice to officially meet ya." Her English has an Irish tone creating both a comforting and exotic manner. The splash of tan freckles scattered across her rosebud nose and fair cheeks give her a youthful glow.

"Nice to finally meet you too."

"Grand! It will be the best summer. The other student went to grab a fizzy drink, but he should be right back. Then we'll be off!"

She shuffles through a stack of papers in a substantial portfolio.

"Oomph!" Fiona sways on her heels.

"Sorry, ma'am." A large man with two big suitcases and a small dog carrier gives an apologetic wave as the portfolio falls from Fiona's hands, sending a cascade of papers floating around the passing crowd.

I'm scooping sheets off the floor when I spot the student list. Students from all over the world fill the ten program slots, and three are from the US. In one of our phone conversations, Fiona mentioned that one of the US students is meeting us in Dublin since his family decided to make a vacation out of it. Which leaves two of us on this flight.

I pause on a familiar name: *Finn Connolly.*

My breath catches. *No, it can't be. That would be crazy.*

Just to be sure, I run my finger down the column next to his name. Butterflies are already fluttering circles in my stomach. St. Joseph's, Bethesda, MD.

The memories come flooding back before I can stop them. The middle of junior year—one day he was here and the next gone. The rumors and gossip around school said that Finn transferred to be closer to his dad's job at NIH in Bethesda. I don't know how many Finn Connolly's there are in Bethesda, Maryland, but there can't be many.

Just as this realization is settling in, Fiona interrupts my thoughts.

"Teagan, I'd like ya to meet Finn Connolly."

As I turn, stomach somersaulting, my eyes lock with the same deep caramel eyes that used to haunt my dreams.

He's the one thing I'm not prepared for.

Chapter Two

The engine revs as we speed down the runaway, my heart matching each acceleration. Knots twist my stomach as the wheels leave the ground. Knowing I have no control of this is terrifying. I close my eyes, like I do every time I fly, and force myself to think about landing in Ireland. All the stress of flying will be worth it. In about seven hours, we will be in Dublin and all my plans for the summer will become a reality.

After what seems like forever, the flight attendant comes over the speaker and announces that we are at cruising height. My eyes need a moment to adjust, but when they do, I catch Finn looking at me, a mix of questions and humor in his gaze.

I shift in my seat and have the urge to call Kayleigh. She would understand the implication of all this. My reputation as the most logical sister seems to disappear when it comes to anything to do with the heart. Kayleigh was there for me when my heart was breaking into pieces over Finn.

"What?" I ask him, a little more abruptly than I intend.

"Do you do that every time you fly?"

"I get a little nervous during takeoff, that's all." I give him my best, most confident, I've-got-everything-under-control smile. "Have you looked over the itinerary?"

His forehead creases slightly at my change of subject but he lets it go. "Yeah, I was just going over it. Looks like we should get some sleep on the flight. It's gonna be a packed day when we land."

Get some sleep? Yeah, right. I'm sitting next to Finn Connolly, closer to him than I've been in over a year and a half. Every time I look at him, my heart starts galloping like a runaway horse.

"I don't think I can sleep on a plane."

"She doesn't have any trouble," Finn says with a nod behind us.

Following the soft murmuring, I glance between the seats and see Fiona already sleeping with a pink satin neck pillow and eye mask. She doesn't seem to be the least bit perturbed about sleeping next to the burly man in a faded U2 T-shirt, playing drums on the seat tray as music blares from his ear buds.

A small laugh escapes my lips before I turn back to the green leather portfolio Fiona gave us at the airport. Embossed with the Emeral Isle logo, it contains all the program information. I trace my finger over the graphic before I flip through the folder. Dividers separate our trip itinerary, university information and dorm assignments, course calendar, important dates, and an ending section on Irish history and culture.

Scanning the room assignments, I find my roommate— a girl named Zoey Campbell from Montreal, Canada. My parents took us to Montreal last summer. I loved everything about the city— the incredible Aura show at the Notre-Dame Basilica, the variety of plants and art at the Montreal Botanical Gardens, and the cosmopolitan feel of walking the cobblestone streets and dining at the European inspired cafes. I could have stayed a lot longer than the week we were there for my parent's veterinary conference. Walking with my sisters while our parents attended different seminars came with a certain freedom. Even if we had to stay within a designated area, we had a taste of what college and adulthood would be. Only once did Kayleigh and I have to go out looking for Ashling, who decided to follow along with a street artist. Knowing Ashling's tendency to roam, we considered ourselves very lucky.

The memory settles my nerves and I grin at the thought of living on my own for the first time. My heartbeat finally slows as I leaf through the organized setup. Plans are good. Feeling grounded once more, I chance a look Finn's way.

He's absorbed in the Irish history portion of the material. There's a cute wrinkling around his eyes as he pushes a few strands of blond hair away. He has that Chris Hemsworth look, strong for sure but also intelligent and funny. No wonder he was so popular in school. Finn has a presence about him.

He and his family moved to Maryland in the middle of our sophomore year from…well, I'm not sure exactly where. His dad is a four-star admiral in the US Navy. He was honored for his work on terrorism during the war and in scientific research, which ended up being vital to intelligence during the war. No one knew what his dad was researching since it was classified, but whatever it was, his role ultimately saved thousands of lives. His dad's research and military position eventually led him to NIH, and ultimately Finn's abrupt departure from school.

Finn's eyes meet mine, and I realize I've been staring at him while lost in thought. Heat floods my cheeks as his smile quirks up on one side. I avert my gaze to the window, where a watercolor of orange, yellow, and red combine to create a masterpiece in the sky.

"Wow," I say, forgetting my embarrassment for the moment.

"It's incredible, isn't it? No matter how many times I fly, it never gets old." He leans over to get a better look out the window, bringing his face within inches of mine. Pine and peppermint tickle my nose, and I find myself leaning into him ever so slightly before catching myself and pulling back.

"So, have you been to Ireland before?" I'm trying to regain my footing.

He leans back into his seat. "Yeah, a few times. My dad was stationed in County Cork, close to where the old Navy Air Station was in Queenstown. They have a small research center there now, and he was deployed there for a year. Actually, that's where we went when I left Forest Haven."

"Oh, I thought you went somewhere by NIH for your dad's job."

Finn groans and shakes his head. "I'm so ready for all the lies to stop. You have any idea what it's like to always have to hide everything? It makes it hard to remember what's the truth sometimes."

His response takes me by surprise. I don't know what to say, so I give him an encouraging smile, hoping he will continue.

"A lot of my dad's work is 'top secret.'" Finn snorts a little at this. "So, we told everyone that's where I was going, but we actually came to Ireland. I had to lie to everyone and break…friendships."

A flash of anger lights his eyes. "My dad does work at NIH though, that is true. He was just needed in Ireland for a part of the research. But his team is in Maryland."

"That must be hard." I tread the line carefully. "You didn't want to leave Forest Haven?"

His eyes grow intense. "No."

So much is packed into that word. My mind travels to April Jenkins, his girlfriend at the time. The golden couple. Could he be thinking of her?

"Do you ever talk to anyone from Forest Haven?" Now I'm inching into an area I'm not sure I want to know about.

"No." He frowns. "That's the hardest part about being Admiral Connolly's son. He's my dad, but his job always comes first, regardless of how it messes with my life." The tiniest ounce of bitterness edges his tone.

"Everyone missed you when you left school."

He looks into my eyes, questions swimming in the depths of that caramel. "It was hard to leave. But without leaving…"

We're quiet for a moment, questions and memories lingering in the air between us. Finally, he draws a breath. "So, you never gave up on this program, huh?"

"You remember I wanted this program?"

"Teagan." He laughs and raises one eyebrow. "You talked about it all the time in chemistry. Of course, I remember."

A warmth spreads through me knowing he hadn't forgotten me.

"Actually," he says, "I probably should thank you. I don't think I would have considered applying for Emerald Isle if it wasn't for you."

"Oh." *He was thinking of me.*

"You never told me what made you want to apply for the program though."

"My parents," I say quickly, thankful for something to ground me once more. "They actually met at Emerald Isle, in this special veterinary co-op program between Emerald Isle and their magnet school in Maryland. They spent the first four years in Ireland and then the next four on the eastern shore of Maryland. My parents fell in love at Emerald Isle, and the rest is history."

The same glow warms me every time I think of their love story. Like a fairytale that never gets old. I hope one day I will be able to tell my own story, and it will be just as special.

"Really? That's awesome." He looks surprised and genuinely intrigued. "I guess Ireland is a magical place. Anything can happen, right?"

His lips pull into a lopsided smile, and all the emotions I'd felt in school come flooding back. Just like that I know my heart doesn't stand a chance.

~

Flickering lights make my eyes twitch. I squeeze them tighter, not wanting to get up yet. I curl into my pillow, and drift back to sleep.

The flight attendant's voice comes over the speaker. "We are preparing for landing. Please bring your seats to the full upright position."

Landing? My head shoots up, and light assaults my eyes. Pulling myself upright, I realize that I am resting not on a pillow, but on Finn. Horrified, I run a hand through my tangled hair, the scent of pine and peppermint tempting me to bring a few strands to my nose. Finn sends me a sleepy grin, his eyes landing on my cheek. I instinctively reach up to cover the mark left by his shoulder.

"As we begin our final descent, keep your seatbelts fastened. We may hit some turbulence," the young flight attendant chimes, seemingly without a worry in the world. "If you look out your window, you will see beautiful Dublin. Even in the rain, it sparkles like a gem. Today's forecast calls for more rain and a warm eighteen degrees Celsius, or sixty-four degrees Fahrenheit for us Americans." She gives a wink, and a low rumble of laughter sweeps the cabin. I mentally thank my parents again for the rain jacket.

I shriek as the plane dips and my stomach somersaults.

"It's just some turbulence." Finn tries to offer assurance, but the plane swerves to the side, bumping like a bike on a rocky, root-gnarled trail. Each dip and rise tightens my grip on the armrest. After one deceptively large plunge, I let out another screech and realize I'm not gripping the armrest but Finn's hand.

Seriously, what is wrong with me? I gravitate toward him like a moth to a flame. Like mud to a white horse. Like our dog, Jack, to my mom's roast beef. *Okay, that's it! Keep thinking of similes. That's better than thoughts of impending doom.*

The plane suddenly nosedives, and all of my social etiquette and hesitation fly out the window. I squeeze Finn's hand, burrow my head into his shoulder. It feels not just safe, but familiar. A strong arm wraps around me and my head nestles against his chest, his steady, rhythmic breaths calming me. His chin rests on my head and I close my eyes, letting him comfort me, while I try to think of anything other than crashing to the ground.

And that's when the memory hits. When Finn came into our classroom for the first time, mid-sophomore year, Ms. Adams asked me to be his lab partner. I gladly took her up on this as my current partner, Julia Webb, was not too keen on doing anything other than gossiping about boys. She certainly didn't want to invest much effort into our labs. I didn't mind doing all of the work, I kind of preferred it that way—at least I knew I would get a good grade. But her incessant talking grated on my nerves. Don't get me wrong. Julia was nice enough, but I actually wanted to learn, which was not one of her goals. So, I figured anyone else would be better than listening to her endless chatter.

And then I saw Finn. I mean, I really looked at him. He wasn't just cute. The guy was almost too cute to be real. Around six feet tall with sandy blond hair framing a strong, chiseled face, he would have looked too old for high school if not for his worn jeans and faded red Manchester United hoodie. His appearance shouted confident athlete, star of the football team, but his smile whispered an intelligent kindness. From the very first moment our eyes locked, there was something special between us—something that drew us together.

Despite my initial attraction, my feelings about him weren't confirmed until we had our first lab together. He was not the silent partner I hoped for after Julia, but rather an active participant who knew what he was doing. And what's more, I could tell he not only enjoyed the lab but also found chemistry and science interesting. To have a lab partner who actually wanted to discuss science was a welcome change, but it was more than that. I felt I'd found a kindred spirit in Finn.

We worked seamlessly together on that first lab, like we were made for each other—well, at least made to be lab partners, but a more romantic partnership did pass through my mind a time or two. I found over the course of the next few weeks that it wasn't just a feeling. Where my weaknesses in data computation became evident, Finn easily led us through it together. Where he lacked precision at some of the finer measurements and procedures, I shone, bringing him right along with me. We complimented each other and helped each other improve where we were weakest.

I reached the point where I was counting down the hours till chemistry every day and I couldn't fool myself that it was just because of the content anymore. I was looking forward to seeing Finn. I looked forward to being with him. While we mainly focused on chemistry, some details of our lives inevitably came out, like how we were both big fans of The Brazen Heads, a quirky Irish band that I recognized Finn humming one day as we worked.

I actively looked for him throughout the day and thought about him way more than I should have, especially considering I was dating Scott. Scott Anderson and I have known each other our entire lives. We teased each other in elementary school, avoided each other in middle school, and finally discovered what we thought were romantic feelings for each other during our freshman year. He asked me to the Spring Fling, and we stayed together the next two years. I really liked Scott, but I never felt any of the electricity or magnetism I felt when I was around Finn. While I enjoyed being with Scott and had fun when we were together, I never counted down the hours (or minutes) to seeing him. Chemistry was the last period of the day, and sometimes the days seemed so long that I could barely stand the wait to get to class and see Finn. While it was nice to see Scott, I needed to see Finn.

One Friday toward the end of January, the end of Finn's first month at Forest Haven, we were staying late in the lab when Scott came to the door. We were planning on joining some of his friends from the swim team at the local diner and then we were going to see a movie. I wished something would come up to get me out of the date, but Finn jumped in before I could say anything, telling me to go ahead with Scott and he would finish cleaning up for us. I felt as if he said, "no problem." He brushed it off, but I could tell there was more going on, more not being said. When I caught his eye, there was the briefest flash of something unnerving in his expression, but it was quickly covered up with his friendly smile. I knew in that moment that my feelings for Finn were much stronger than I had realized.

A collective scream breaks through the memory as the plane bumps onto the runway, wheels touching down like a stone skipping on the water and skidding in a half circle until the plane finally stops.

"Well, we're off to a good start," Finn jokes. "Can't wait to see what the rest of the trip has in store.

Chapter Three

The Dublin airport passes in a blur as Fiona leads through check-in, currency exchange, and baggage.

"Have a nice visit and hope ya find yer treasure," the attendant says, stamping my passport.

Find my treasure. Must be how they greet visitors to Ireland.

We follow Fiona along the corridor. Conversations surround us. "And don't worry, most people around here speak an Irish English, which is a bit of a mix of the two. So many people comin' and goin', you'll get used to it."

We meet our fellow US student on the outdoor rotunda. When I first see Kyle Johnson, I mistake him for an NFL player. He has an all-American look to him, curly blond hair, blue eyes, and a dimple when he smiles. While I've never felt tall, standing between Finn and Kyle I feel absolutely tiny. Both are just over six feet, but Finn is leaner than Kyle, who I learn did actually play football—a left tackle on his San Diego high school team. His letterman jacket has so many pins that he looks like an outright football hero.

"And they will have plenty of time to explore durin' in-dependent study," Fiona explains with great excitement, but Kyle's mom's face creases and her bottom lip trembles.

Kyle puts a gentle arm around his mom and gives her shoulder a squeeze. "It'll be great. Couldn't be a safer place."

His overall cheerful tone is enough to bring a small smile to the curve of her lips.

"So, where are you guys from?" he asks as we move off to the side, leaving his mom and Fiona to continue their conversation.

"Maryland," Finn and I say at the same time.

"Oh, are you guys together?"

"No," I blurt out. "We're not together."

Kyle raises an eyebrow. "Okay, just meant that since you're both from Maryland you might know each other, but my bad."

Finn studies me before responding. "We did go to school together," he tells Kyle without taking his eyes off me. "We were chemistry partners."

Before I can say anything, Kyle groans. "Chemistry was my nemesis. I needed it to keep up my science GPA for the engineering program, but man, it almost killed me. Luckily, I made it through and was able to get into the program, but it was close."

"Yeah, I get that. MLA formatting was my nemesis, but chemistry was…" Finn pauses to look at me. "Fun."

"Yeah, chemistry was the most memorable part of high school," I say softly. "I've always loved science, but chemistry was…" I hesitate to think of an appropriate word for what it was. "Special."

And now it's my turn to look intently at Finn. He matches my gaze. The tension between us is building.

"Well, you guys must have had a good teacher. Mine was seriously a mad scientist. Wouldn't be surprised if he was all Breaking Bad when not at school."

"I'm goin' grab a taxi and then we'll be on our way!" Fiona calls to us.

Kyle runs over for a last goodbye with his parents, leaving Finn and me together with the luggage at our feet.

My cell phone rings, and when I pull it from my bag, Scott's name and photo stare back me. I send it to voicemail and slip the phone back in my bag.

"So, you and Scott still together?" Finn's gaze drifts to the ground as he kicks a rock.

"No. We actually broke up in the end of junior year."

Finn kicks at another rock.

"We realized we're better as friends. But I think I'd always known that."

He's looking at me now. "Teagan, do you think—"

"Alright, we're all set." Fiona's back already.

No! Do I think what? I want to scream it, but I am still relatively sane, so I hold myself back. A mix of disappointment and relief flash over Finn's face, and we follow Fiona to the taxi.

Our driver, Michael, shakes hands with both of us, then slides his tweed cap back on his bald head. "First time in Ireland?"

"Yes." I smile. "I'm so happy to finally be here."

Michael nods in a knowing way. "Aye. Hope ya find yer treasure, lass."

Treasure again. What is it with everyone saying that? I'm about to ask when he turns to Finn.

"Not my first time. I actually lived in County Cork for a bit. My dad's in the US navy."

"G'wan!" Michael grins. "A fella following in his footsteps, eh."

Finn's jaw clenches. "Something like that."

Michael strolls to the driver's seat. "Let's head to the bog."

After a surprising number of stops along the way, we're cutting it close on making it to the university in time.

Michael, as nice as he is, doesn't seem to have much of an idea of time management. He stopped while passing anyone he knew—and even one man he didn't know, but apparently the guy had great looking sheep.

I find it disconcerting for the car to be winding down the road on the left side. Everything feels off, and I keep pushing the floor like a brake.

"You okay?" Kyle asks.

"Oh, yeah. Just takes a little getting used to the driving."

That crooked grin again…the one that turns my insides into a big tangle. "You keep twisting your necklace, and I think it may be wearing thin."

"Oh." I let the chain drop back to my chest.

"My mom would love that necklace. She really likes emeralds."

"Me too. My parents gave it to me for my birthday.

"Aye, emeralds are a funny thing around these parts." Michael speaks up, a twinkle in his eye—an eye directed at me, not the road. Feeling the urge to reach for my poor necklace again, I slide my hands under my legs.

"Many, many tales." Fiona shakes her head.

"All right." Kyle grins. "Tell us a good one."

"That'd have to be the Kildare Stone." Michael turns around to grin at us.

Please keep your eyes on the road.

"Right." Fiona sighs.

"Okay, I'm intrigued." Kyle sits up straighter. "What's this legend?"

Fiona turns around, eyes twinkling. "Ya must know people 'round here take legends very seriously. It's not just a story but a part of the culture."

She waits for us to nod before continuing.

"Legend has it that there is an emerald, larger than any Irishman has ever seen, hidden on a farm in a small town in Kildare."

"From the time of the druids?" Kyle leans forward and rests his elbows on his knees.

"Nah, this is a modern legend. One that began only about fifty years ago. But as tends to happen around these parts, the best of tales become legends quickly."

"Why do people believe it's hidden in Kildare?" Finn asks.

"I heard it from my own da." Michael turns around, causing the little car to swerve on the bumpy road. "One night he was with the lads at O'Shea's, havin' a pint, mindin' their own, when this bloody man by the name of Eamon told the entire pub. The gift of gab he had. One of his farmhands had a fifteen-carat emerald, brought over from Columbia. They thought he was gas. Who comes to Ireland with that kind of stone? Says before the family left to go back to Columbia, he gave him the emerald as a grand gesture of thanks. Grandest I've ever heard of."

"But didn't you say no one knows where it is? That it's hidden somewhere on a farm?" I ask.

"Ah, that's right lass. You see, the loon didn't keep the stone. He claims to have buried it somewhere on his land. Crazy eejit."

"Someone must have seen him or noticed something," Finn says.

"Not a one."

"If it's true, then that emerald must be worth a fortune." Kyle rubs his chin.

"Emerald that size, and one from Columbia, could be around a million Euros," Fiona says.

"And he buried it in the ground? Why would he do that?" Kyle asks.

"Superstition," Michael and Fiona say together.

"He believed it was bad luck to keep it?" Finn's blue eyes are found as the proverbial saucers.

"More cursed I'd say." Michael seems very serious for the first time since we met him.

"Money is the root of all evil, or so he believed. Swore it kept him up at night."

"Crazy." Kyle sighs.

"That's not the craziest part," Fiona says. "There's a map."

"So, somewhere there's a map that could lead to an actual treasure?" Kyle asks.

"'Tis the legend."

It doesn't make sense. "I would've thought people would have tried to find it over the years. It can't still be there."

"Oh, they tried." Michael gives a chuckle. "Folks say Eamon stood guard, shootin' at anyone who tried to enter his property. Catching a few at that."

"Could this all just be the story of a crazy man?" Finn asks.

Michael and Fiona merely shrug.

We pull up to the university, and the boys get out first to help with the luggage.

"Thank you, Michael. It's been an interesting ride."

"No bother, lass." As I'm climbing out, he adds, "Hope ya find yer treasure."

His words catch me by surprise, and I stumble before giving a quick wave goodbye.

Treasure.

With the legend still on my mind, a real-life treasure hunt doesn't seem too far-fetched anymore.

⌒

At Emerald Isle, we go straight to the Meet and Greet in a main level conference room. We are the last to arrive, but everyone greets us warmly. We have just enough time to grab a corned beef sandwich and brownie before the program director speaks.

The same man I saw three years ago walks to the podium. He's leaning a little more on his walking stick, but his plaid pants and sweater vest are right in place. He's missing his hat today though, and his red hair is peppered with more grey than I remember.

"Welcome." He looks around the room. "Ye have all shown great scientific achievement and potential to be offered a position in our Science Research Scholars Program." He pauses as a round of applause sounds. "Hope ye continue to grow within this program and at the end, be better scientists for it. May the luck of the Irish serve you well." He winks and another round of applause sounds.

This is real. I'm suddenly overwhelmed with reality of what's happening. *I'm in the program* and will be spending the summer in Ireland. And most importantly, at the end I may have the opportunity to stay at Emerald Isle and continue with the research. I promise myself that no matter what else happens over these next couple of months, I will do everything I can to win the position at the end.

"Hi, I'm Sarah Murray, your student affairs representative. I recently graduated from Emerald Isle. I was in your position just five years ago, and my partner and I were lucky enough to have our research topic chosen. Applying to this program was the best decision I ever made. I came here from the US, but I don't think I'll ever leave Ireland!"

A round of good-hearted laughter sounds. "Okay, now let's get to it. I'll be spending the next few minutes going over some of the program highlights and dorm rules."

Sarah speaks about everything from shared bathrooms to the dining plan for the week. I follow along on the printout, but my mind wanders to someone from whom I should be keeping my distance. He's a distraction I don't need right now.

"Tomorrow morning you'll get your team assignments, which is always an exciting moment." Sarah smiles. "You and your partner will receive your assigned on-site locations and will work together throughout this week, getting to know each other as you learn about science research foundations and the rules and procedures for the summer research. You will check in routinely with your mentor at the university. Your mentor will be an invaluable asset to you as well as your on-location supervisor."

I catch Finn's eye across the patio before turning my attention back to Sarah. Tomorrow we'll find out our partners.

"So, now you have time to drop off any belongings to your assigned dorm room and freshen up a bit before we head over to O'Callahan's Pub for a friendly dinner with live Irish music!"

Another cheer goes up before we exit to the halls. Glancing at the university map, I follow the path to the dorms. When I reach my room, my roommate is already there.

"Hi! I'm Teagan. It looks like we're rooming together!" I greet her a little too brightly. *Ugh, why do I sound like a freshman all over again?* Like I'm trying too hard to be with the in-crowd. I already made that mistake once, best not repeat it. And let's be honest, I was never meant for the in-crowd anyway.

"Hi, Teagan. I'm Zoey." She gives me a hug, and I'm reminded of Kayleigh. Not in appearance but in the feeling I get from being around her. She's shorter than me, probably about five-foot-three with fluffy, light blond hair that falls just below her shoulders. Her grey eyes are friendly and her smile warm. I get the feeling we're going to be quick friends.

"You have a preference?" She points to the two single beds sitting on either side of a large window, which could provide lots of natural light if the rain ever stops.

"Either's good with me."

"All right, I'll take this one." Zoey tosses her duffle bag on the bed to the right. "It's kinda bare in here, huh?"

Looking around the room, I have to agree. It's compact, but functional. Two desks stand across from each other on our corresponding walls, an empty bulletin board above each. Two small dressers await our clothing, although I will probably keep mine in my suitcase, since I have it organized by daily activity.

"So, you're from the US, eh?"

"Yeah." I take a seat on the edge of my bed. "Maryland. You're from Canada?"

"Montreal. Oh, how was your flight? I heard the flight from Australia was quite the bumpy ride."

How do I explain the flight? The terror. The anxiety. And…the best sleep I've had in a long time. "It was ok," I finally say. "Yours?"

"Slept like a log." Her smile is the epitome of content. "I really want a shower more than anything right now."

I glance at the clock, feeling every bit as grungy as Zoey. "I think we can do it. Ten minutes each and we should make it. You go first."

Zoey jumps up. "I'll be quick!"

The bathroom door opens about eight minutes later, not that I'm keeping track or anything, and Zoey comes out looking adorable in black jeans and a white puffy-sleeved shirt. Her heart-shaped face is shining with renewed energy and enthusiasm.

"Your turn." She beams at me while slipping on black feather earrings.

The hot water feels so good that I almost forget about my time limit. Stepping out of the shower, I feel invigorated—clean and ready to take on the world.

That's better. I nod at myself in the foggy mirror. *Much fresher.* I pull on my black jeans and baby-blue, long-sleeved satin blouse. I apply a little black eye liner and mascara, making my bright blue eyes stand out against the darkness. A few swipes of peach blush and a little lip gloss, and I feel like a new person. I slip on my gold-mesh dangle earrings and emerald claddagh necklace.

"You look amazing!" Zoey gushes as I come out of the bathroom. "I bet you don't even have to dry your hair, do you? It probably is just perfection on its own. If I didn't dry my hair, it would be a frizzy mess, which it probably will be anyway, the moment we go back out in the rain."

"Oh, stop. You look beautiful." I laugh as she does a twirl. "And we need to get going." I quickly tie my still-damp hair into a smooth ponytail that falls down the middle of my back.

"Let's go."

Thankful that I have totally lucked out in the roommate department, my mood is bright by the time we make it to the conference hallway. Maybe this luck will continue?

I have thought about Finn almost every other second since I saw his name on the student list, but when I catch a glimpse of him in the conference room, I'm not ready to see him again.

"Oomph." Zoey bumps into me. "Why'd you stop?"

Before I can answer, she follows my gaze towards Finn. There's an intensity as he stares back at me, not moving a muscle until Kyle bumps him in the shoulder, clearly telling yet another of his comical stories.

"Okay, what's going on?" Zoey turns on me. I guess I wasn't the only one to notice. "Is there something going on between—"

"No," I say, interrupting her. "He's just a guy I used to know in school. It's nothing."

She raises her eyebrow, looking like she doesn't believe a word of it, but thankfully lets it drop.

"Hey, Teagan, over here!" Kyle calls from across the room.

Walking towards them, I try to keep my eyes averted from Finn, and in doing so, notice Kyle gaping at Zoey. I almost laugh out loud at his mouth literally gapes open.

"Kyle, Finn, this is Zoey, my roommate." I aim the introduction directly at Kyle.

"Hey." Kyle reaches out a hand to Zoey.

Zoey's bright smile matches his, her cheeks all rosy and eyes twinkling.

"Think they even know we're here?" Finn whispers in my ear, his breath tickling my neck. A faint scent of soap lingers as he pulls away. He's wearing jeans and a black button-down shirt, revealing a silver Celtic cross on a black cord.

"Nope." I laugh nervously. "We disappeared the moment they saw each other."

Finn's eyes trail down my face, seemingly taking in every detail.

"Okay, time to head over to O'Callahan's!" Sarah announces.

We follow her onto an ancient cobblestone path, Finn and I trailing a little behind Kyle and Zoey, who are still immersed in conversation—and each other.

"I think we have front row seats to the often-talked-about-but-never-actually-witnessed love at first sight." I nod toward them.

"I do believe you're right." We share a look of amusement before he gets serious again. "I take it you don't believe in love at first sight?"

Heat prickles my face as memories of seeing Finn for the first-time flash through my mind.

"Ah, I don't know. I mean, no. Of course not, you can't fall in love with someone the first time you see them. That's not love."

"I'll give you that, but don't you think there can be a special something between people that just met?

"Sure," I say, narrowing my eyes. "Attraction, but that's not love."

When he doesn't respond, I continue. "Don't tell me you believe in love at first sight?"

A smile teases his lips. "I think I do."

"What? Seriously? And you're a man of science." I give his arm a playful push.

Finn shrugs. "Experiments may not be able to prove the theory, but it can't disprove it either."

"Okay, first be careful using 'prove' about anything in science. You know that. Remember we support or don't support a hypothesis, but—"

"Teagan, not everything can be explained with science. You can't categorize love in some data table. It's more than that."

We stand at the door to the pub while the rest of the group passes us.

"How do you know?"

He takes a deep breath, but before he can answer, Fiona leans out the door.

"Come on, you two! Tables are fillin' up." She narrows her eyes and smiles in a conspiring way. "And if you're plottin' a treasure hunt, you wouldn't be the first after hearin' the legend. But I warn ya, nothin' good has ever come of it."

And with that, we follow her inside, all thoughts of love and treasure fading away.

Chapter Four

It's everything I ever imagined an Irish pub would be—fun, welcoming, and completely authentic. Since it's evening, everyone is a little more dressed up than would be common for a midday meal or football game (soccer, not American football). Booming laughter rumbles from the bar and friendly conversation buzzes all around. A four-person band is setting up in one of the corners as people shift chairs in their direction. A man who looks to be in his early thirties is tuning a fiddle while simultaneously balancing a pint in his hand.

We find Kyle and Zoey at a table close to the band and slide in next to them. They're already huddled together looking over a menu, leaving Finn and me to share the other menu on the table.

"I'm going with the fish and chips." I pass Finn the menu, hoping to put space between us. Yet when I slide closer to Zoey, I immediately miss the warmth of our connection.

"He's incredible," Zoey whispers in my ear.

"Yeah, he is," I murmur, glancing at Finn. When she doesn't respond, I see her watching Kyle place our orders at the bar.

"You guys seem to be hitting it off."

"Yes! It's crazy. I never expected any of this." There's a new sparkle in her eyes and her excitement is contagious. I know she's referring to things with Kyle, but she reminds me that just being here is a gift.

"Hey, the bartender needs our IDs," Kyle tells us as a Colin Farrell look-a-like heads our way.

"How's the form?" he asks when he reaches our table. "Need to see yer IDs."

Luckily Kayleigh bought me an Irish slang book when I found out I would be in Ireland this summer. We have been practicing together over the past few weeks and I feel like a student again, perched on the edge of the seat happily prepared. "How's the form?" is a phrase we practiced regularly in our mock conversations. It basically means, "How's it going?" I can't hold the smile back thinking of Ashling's expression when we asked her at home. She thought we were losing our minds.

I hand him my ID, new from my recent eighteenth birthday.

"Cute." He winks at me before taking Finn's ID.

Being a rule follower, I have been waiting until my twenty-first birthday for my first drink. The thought of losing control sets me on edge. On the rare times I was around people drinking, I always felt uncomfortable and could never imagine getting drunk like some of my classmates. However, here in this pub in Ireland seems like the time to have one if I'm going to. And I don't have to worry about it being illegal since the drinking age is eighteen years old here. Just as I'm thinking this, I see Zoey's face fall.

"I don't turn eighteen until July," she tells him.

"Sorry, lass. No exceptions. Could cost me my job. Is it the black stuff for the rest of ya?"

We all agree on Guinness, while Zoey slumps in her seat, deflated.

"No worries, Zo. We'll celebrate big next month. A big birthday bash." There's a gleam in Kyle's eyes. I'm certain he's already forming a plan, and whatever it is, it will be nothing short of spectacular.

"Thanks, Kyle." Zoey smiles at him, apparently noticing the same.

The bartender returns with our drinks. He sends me his gorgeous side-smile and I feel my cheeks warm, not from attraction but rather a ridiculous sense of unwanted attention and awkwardness because of Finn. *Seriously, why do I feel like we're together when there's nothing really between us?*

Because that's a lie and I know it. We may not be together, but there is definitely something between us.

"Name's Seamus." The bartender slides the pints onto the table. "The guys settin' up over there are cousins of mine, so if there's somethin' ya want to hear, just let me know." He gives me another of his charming winks before heading back to the bar.

"Well, Teagan, I think you have an admirer." Zoey giggles.

"Now, I'm not a lady," Kyle says, "but he's quite the strapping fellow."

The three of us laugh while Finn's face hardens. "You don't want to be distracted from the research this summer," he grumbles.

"I don't know," Zoey says, smiling at Kyle. "I think some distractions are a good thing."

"Not if you're serious about winning the research position."

Zoey doesn't respond. She's gone back to whispering with Kyle.

"I don't plan on letting anything or anyone distract me from the research position." I look Finn pointedly in the eye.

His expression is unreadable. Some kind of mixture of pride and annoyance and something else.

"*Slainte!*" A group of scholar students call from a nearby table.

"*Slainte!*" We raise our glasses back to them.

I take a drink and immediately cough. I don't know what I was expecting, but Guinness is much thicker than I had imagined. Almost like syrup.

"You okay?" Zoey rubs my back.

"Yeah, I'm fine." I notice Finn's questioning stare. "It's just my first, that's all."

"First Guinness?" Kyle asks.

"No. Well, yeah, my first Guinness but also my first drink."

Now it's Kyle's turn to cough. "You've never drank any-thing?"

"Nope, never." I'm rather proud of this achievement.

Finn gives me a slight nod, pride definitely winning out in his expression.

I take another sip of the Guinness, the second time feel-ing a little smoother than the first. It's sweet but with a slight bitterness at the end. There's almost a chocolate feel to it, but chocolate aside, I know I will not be drinking the whole pint. I'll count this up to a new experience in Ireland, but not something I will be repeating soon.

The band opens with an upbeat tune, and a few cheers go up. I recognize it as the classic pub song *Whiskey in a Jar.* Seamus catches my eye, a smile growing on his face as he nods to my Guinness. Laughing, I send him a thumbs up. He must see his share of first timers in the pub. Tourists coming from around the world, looking to have their first pint of Guinness in a real Dublin pub.

The jig is upbeat, and a few locals have already joined the small dance floor. The dance steps look natural for both the young and old. And then there are the few students trying their best to keep up, looking as clumsy as newborn colts finding their legs. But they have smiles on their faces, laughing with the locals.

Seamus nods to the dance floor, eyebrows raised.

"Go for it, Teagan!" Zoey nudges me.

I laugh again, which Seamus takes as a yes, and before I know it, I'm swinging around with him on the dance floor, his strong hands holding mine tightly as we hop and spin.

"Just follow me and ya'll be grand," he says, when I trip for the third time.

"I guess I'm not much of a dancer."

"Blarney. Everybody is with the right partner."

An image of dancing with Finn crosses my mind.

Seamus grimaces as I step on his foot again.

I groan. "Sorry. I should stop."

"Nah. Give it a lash."

And I do. I allow myself to let go and just move with Seamus. When the song ends, there's an eruption of cheers.

"You're right. That was so fun. Thank you, Seamus."

"Anytime."

"Not bad for a first timer," a deep voice says from behind us.

"Teagan, this is Ryan McCarthy, another one of O'Callahan's finest."

"Teagan." Ryan reaches for my hand, a black tattoo peeking out from under his shirt sleeve. A tangle of sharp edges resembling an ancient woven crown wraps around his forearm, a snake arching out of the top, its eyes staring straight at me. Letting go of my hand, he nods to the tattoo. "It's a family thing."

"Oh, like a coat of arms?"

A wicked grin spreads across his broad face. "Somethin' like that." He winks at me, and I feel myself taking a step back.

"Ryan moved down from Limerick last year," Seamus explains. "He's been helpin' us on the boat, and I couldn't find a better first mate."

"Aye. Best thing I ever did was move down here. Dublin is happenin'. Get to work with the best lads. Fishin' all day, drinkin' all night." He laughs and nudges me with his elbow.

"Eejit." Seamus nods to a table in the corner. "Charlie's table is up another round."

As Ryan heads off, Seamus leans closer. "Ryan's sound. He went through some rough stuff up north. Doesn't talk about it."

"And you're trying to help him."

Seamus just shrugs. "He's a grand worker and a strong fisherman."

"You're a good guy for helping him."

"Let's get ya back with your mates before ya start spreadin' that 'round."

Irish guys really aren't like any other guys. Something about their dangerous facade and offbeat kindness.

"Ya need anythin', give me a call." Seamus's smile is one in a million, and I have no doubt he has the potential to be a heartbreaker. When he hands me his number on a bar napkin, I slip it into my bag, thinking it's nice to have a friend in Dublin.

"Way to go, Teagan!" A dark-haired girl hoots in her sulky Italian accent from the adjacent table, after Seamus leaves. "He's gorgeous."

My eyes dart to Finn. The muscles around his jaw are clenched tight. I realize everyone must be thinking the same thing. *Agh*. I need to clarify right now.

"No, no." I hold my hands up. "Just friends."

The girl laughs. "Sure, sweetie. Whatever you say."

"Who is she again?" I turn to Zoey, annoyance raking my tone.

"Maria Ferrari. She's from Florence, and from what I can see, she's not all that interested in the research part of the program," Zoey whispers, as she nods in Maria's direction.

Maria is staring intently at Finn, who doesn't seem to notice as he and Kyle debate the upcoming Irish football game.

From the look in her eyes, I think she's found her project this summer. The thought sends my stomach rolling.

~

The next morning, Zoey and I get to the small lecture hall just in time for the beginning of the session. Sarah is standing at the podium, shifting through papers as I gaze around looking for someone I'm not quite ready to admit has already taken up that all-too-familiar spot in my heart.

Zoey giggles. "There's Kyle. Let's sit with them." She nearly drags me over, sliding into the two seats behind them. Kyle and Zoey smile dreamily at each other and I avert my gaze.

Finn nods a greeting. That familiar connection and intimacy we experienced since day one seems to be walled off now. I lean back in my chair to consider this.

The thing is that the timing has never been right for Finn and me. After seeing Scott that fateful day in the lab, there was always this invisible wall between us. No matter how much I wanted to be with him—and that desire grew more and more each day—I was with Scott. Scott was safe and reliable, and even then I knew Finn had the potential to change my whole world. Also, though my feelings were growing stronger and stronger for Finn, I didn't know how he felt and was too scared to ask. Then the summer between sophomore and junior year, I was scrolling on social media and saw a photo that April posted of her and Finn with the caption, "Officially a couple!" It hit me like a soccer ball to the gut.

The beginning of junior year brought Finn and me together again…our Honors Anatomy and Physiology class. We were allowed to choose our lab partners, and our eyes immediately caught one another's, and we were together again. Regardless of our social lives, we always worked well together. His smile was all that was needed to give me hope once more. In the back of my mind, I knew it could all end horribly, but some things are stronger than the mind—as hard as that is for me to admit.

Our first lab brought with it not only a painfully intricate dissection of a pig, but also the familiar give-and-go that made us perfect together—in the lab. Anatomy was first thing in the morning and each day started with so much adrenaline that sometimes I would crash toward the end of the school day, wanting the next day to begin so I could be with Finn again.

Seeing him first thing in the morning allowed me to learn so much more about him, like he's an early riser, just like me. While other students rolled into school with their coffee, half asleep, Finn came in looking like he'd been up for hours, which I found out he had been. One day, he mentioned how he liked to get up early to read before anyone else was up. I had followed that same practice since middle school, so I found myself thinking about him in those early hours while I drank my tea, book open in my hand. The fact that we were so different from most other teenagers was just another thing that made me see how well we fit together.

One morning he texted me at six in the morning. Just two words: "Good morning." My heart seemed set on leaping right out of my chest. I texted back, and it became our thing to be the first person to say good morning each day. I imagined him with his own book and coffee, which made me desperate to be with him.

But it wasn't meant to be.

The last lab we had together was a dissection of a mammalian heart. We were halfway through the dissection after the first day. I waited for Finn on that second day, but he never came in. I checked my email while recording measurements into the graph, but nothing. Figuring he was just home, sick with a cold or something, I tried to push the feeling of dread away. I was getting ready to cut into the aorta when Mr. Jones came over to my lab bench and told me that

Finn would no longer be in class. I could either join another group or finish the lab independently. I chose independently, and as my scalpel cut through the thick membrane, my own heart ripped apart. I walked into the hallway in a daze, my stomach churning and heart pounding. Murmurs of Finn's family moving echoed in my ears.

I texted him, but he never responded. There were no more morning texts, no answers to my questions. If not for the large hole in my heart, Finn might have never existed.

"You have fun last night?"

Finn's voice breaks me from the memory. The sight of him is shocking, as if I'm still seeing an image from the past. Two realities colliding.

"Yeah, it was fun." I force a smile that conflicts with my swirling emotions.

His forehead creases, worry replacing his stony expression. "You okay?"

Am I okay? No, I don't think so. The past day and a half have been an overload of emotions, and I think it's all beginning to catch up with me. Luckily, I'm saved from answering when the lights flash, and Sarah walks up to the podium.

"Good morning, and welcome to the first full day of the science research program. Today we will discuss the foundations of science research and the goals and parameters of the program. Our science research program is centered on the creative pursuit of new knowledge through the process of discovery. It involves methodical inquiry and systematic observation of phenomena. It's the understanding of how and why things work. In addition, it furthers exploration of various areas of study in areas such as biology, chemistry, physics—all leading to improvements in life."

An excited murmur sounds as students actively express their desired areas of study.

"Before we continue with our ideas," Sarah says with a knowing smile, "we have to get into our assigned teams.

After you receive your team assignment, you will have time to discuss your ideas. I have a feeling this will be the best year yet!"

A round of cheers follows. Even with the emotional roller coaster I've been on, it's hard not to get wrapped up in the excitement.

Sarah's smile says she's pleased with the reaction. "This year there are four on-site locations consisting of two three-student teams and two two-student teams. You have been matched with both your team and location based off the questionnaire you filled out with the application."

The moment is here. And even though I knew we would get our assignments today, now it feels too soon, like I need another day or two to prepare. Only this time I'm not preparing for an assignment or lab but preparing my heart for either outcome.

Sarah mimics a drumroll on the podium, and everyone laughs—except me. Humor is the only emotion I don't seem to be feeling right now.

"Team one is Kyle, Maria, and Zoey."

Kyle let's out a whoop and turns around to high-five Zoey.

"Team two is Angelo and Eva."

That's five down, five to go.

"Team three is Chloe, Hans, and Erik."

My entire body flushes with heat. That just leaves…

"And team three is Teagan and Finn."

A quick round of applause signals everyone's excitement for their matching. I clap along with them but can't feel my hands.

"Okay, get together with your team, and I will come around with your on-site locations." Sarah manages to be heard over the excited voices.

The blood pounds in my ears. Could it really be that Finn and I are going to be working together? Just the two of us.

All summer long. The need to pull out my phone and call Kayleigh and Aisling is almost too strong to deny.

Finn climbs up to the seat next to me. Is it what I was wishing for…or what I was dreading? Maybe a little of the two. I look at him and any doubt as to my feelings fall away as I find myself thanking God for putting us together even while knowing he still has the ability to break my heart.

"Looks like we're partners again." His voice holds a slight tremor.

Is he having similar feelings?

Partners again. We're being given a second chance. I never thought I would see Finn again, let alone be partners with him. But here we are almost back where we began.

When Sarah joins us, she hands us each a leather binder with *Brigid's Crossing* embossed on the cover.

Chapter Five

"Okay, we have an hour to go over our on-site placement." I'm talking more to myself than to Finn.

"Let's go outside. Looks like the sun is making a rare appearance."

A golden glow shimmers through the open window. A soft breeze flutters in, bringing with it the earthy scent that comes with the sun after a long rain.

"Sounds good."

We pack up our materials and make our way through the rows of chairs. Two other groups seem to have a similar idea and are heading in the same direction. When we go through the doors, I'm immediately grateful for the change of scenery. The air provides an openness the lecture hall lacks.

Out on the promenade, raindrops cling to the grass, shimmering like a field of diamonds. A few university students throw a frisbee on the lawn. Laughter rings throughout the space.

"The sun feels so good." I sigh, lifting my face toward the warm rays. When I open my eyes, Finn is looking at me in that way that always hits me in the gut.

"Okay, let's go through the binder." I remind myself to stay focused on our work, so there won't be time for any other thoughts. I can't let whatever's happening with Finn distract from the reason I'm here—to learn more about science research and to come up with the winning proposal. As long as I keep that firmly in mind, I should be okay.

We wipe off as much water as we can from a bench before sitting on our rain jackets. I flip to the front page of the binder, where the *Brigid's Crossing* logo takes bold center of attention. It's an intricate weaving of old Celtic font in deep brown, with a woven bent cross between the words, which emulates a rustic old-world charm with a touch of the spiritual.

Finn reads aloud. "Brigid's Crossing is located in Cloverdale Village in County Kildare. The farm has been in the Kavanagh family for centuries, carrying on the legacy of generations of horse breeders."

"I always find it amazing that a place can have so much history. In the US, everything seems new. I mean, we think something's old when it was built in the 1800s. I would love to have a generational home like this. I would love nothing more than to carry on my parents' legacy and keep Claddagh Farm a family farm through the generations."

"That would be amazing. We moved around so much; I never know what to put as my hometown on forms and stuff."

"Do you think your parents will be staying in Maryland now?"

"I don't know." He shrugs. "I doubt it. My dad says he's slowing down and wants to stay there for good, but I just don't see it happening."

"Where would you like to live?"

"Maryland. My time at Forest Haven was my favorite." He smiles at me. "But I think I would have enjoyed Ireland more too if it hadn't been so sudden."

Just the mention of Finn's departure from school causes my emotions to swirl again.

"It looks like St. Patrick made a visit to Kildare too, probably with his connection to St. Brigid." Excitement edges his voice.

Looking under the religious affiliation headline, I continue reading. "Ireland has two main religious groups, split between the Republic of Ireland being primarily Catholic, and Northern Ireland being predominantly Protestant. Kildare has been a bastion of Christianity for nearly sixteen centuries. It is partly in the Roman Catholic archdiocese of Dublin, diocese of Kildare and Leighlin, and the Church of Ireland diocese of Meath and Kildare."

"Can you imagine having to fight to practice your faith?"

"No, it's always been there. We can go to Mass basically whenever we want at home."

"Yeah, and I wonder if it's too easy. We're free to do whatever we like, and so many times we just don't because we're tired or something else comes up."

"I know I'm guilty of that."

"We all are. But to see people dying for their faith, it makes me want to stop being so lazy and do something, you know?"

"Should we storm the battlefield?"

Finn laughs. "You know what I mean."

"Yeah, I do."

I remember that Finn has always had an active faith, one where you don't just go through the motions. He has this way of calling others to arms over injustices and leading them in a fight for political truth and action. His passion is one of the things that has always attracted me to him.

"They list a St. Patrick's parish in Cloverdale. Maybe we can check it out?"

When was the last time I actually went to Mass or any service with a clear mind and open heart and not just because I was supposed to? "Sure, I'd love that."

I flip to the binder section on County Kildare and begin reading.

"County Kildare is located in the province of Leinster in the Irish midlands. Kildare is generally flat, being an inland county, but has small hills throughout. Its highest points are the foothills of Wicklow Mountains and the hills north of Kildare town, and those to the west of Kilcock." I continue skimming the county facts. "Oh, Kildare is famous worldwide for its horse racing, home to the Curragh course."

"I'm sure that reminds you of home."

"Yeah, it does." My parents rescued many horses from the racetrack. It's not the sport of racing we have an issue with…it's the treatment and care of the horses that is concerning. Maryland boasts more horses per square acre than any other US state. We host the Preakness States, one of three races in the triple crown. There are off-track thoroughbred racehorses always in need of a home when their career ends early due to injuries or poor performance. My parents have always had a soft spot for them, and the majority of our rescue horses are past racers.

"It says that Brigid's Crossing is home to a multitude of rescue animals, including horses. Looks like they have a similar idea as your family."

I remember Sarah saying we would be placed with partners and locations based on our surveys and background. I now see why I was selected for this location. The question is, why were Finn and I paired? Is our connection that obvious, even on paper?

"I hope so," I say quietly, unable to fathom the thought that the farm is run any way other than the caring way I've grown up. "I'm surprised you remember my family's farm."

"Why would you be surprised? Every time I see a horse, I think of you."

My heart skips at his words, and then anger begins to creep up. "I wouldn't think you would think of me at all."

He looks taken aback. "Why? You were one of my best friends back then."

"One of your best friends? Oh, one who you never told you were leaving? A friend whose calls and texts you never answered. You just left without so much as a 'see ya later.'" I stand up, nervous energy spiraling through my limbs. "You know, I had to finish the heart dissection on my own."

Surprise and regret fill Finn's eyes. "Teagan, I—let me explain."

"You don't need to explain. You left without so much as a goodbye. That's fact."

"It's always about the facts and calculations, isn't it?" Finn stands, the bench creaking with the sudden movement. "The facts you talk about are only what you see. Subjective observations. Sometimes there's more to consider than just the facts."

"Something science can't explain, right? Did I get that right?"

He presses his lips together and takes a step away from me. "Science isn't everything, Teagan. And we aren't in some experiment—we're human, and that means there's more than just 'the facts.' You would understand that if you'd let me explain."

He's looking at me with hopeful eyes now, and while I'm scared to hear his reasons, this is a moment I have been wanting for so long—to learn why he left without a word. Before I can say anything, the bell rings, signaling our time is up and we need to report back to the lecture hall.

"We need to go." I start packing my bag.

"Let's finish this conversation later, okay?"

Without looking at him, I give a brief nod.

As I turn toward the door, my bag catches on the bench, spilling my notebook and phone.

"At least it didn't break." I retrieve the phone.

Finn remains quiet as he stares at a folded napkin. Seamus' phone number. "Don't want to lose this," he grumbles, handing me the napkin and notebook, eyes clouded once more.

We walk back to the lecture hall in silence, both of us leaving things unspoken.

~

Kayleigh and I miss each other's calls all week. It's frustrating, but the time difference and schedules make it nearly impossible to talk. Our sisters group text is going strong, though. Kayleigh's advice is as calming and delicate as I knew it would be, even over text.

"It will all work out in its own time," and *"You guys have all summer. Just let things happen naturally."* While good advice, I am surprisingly leaning towards Ashling's, *"Just rip it off like a bandage and talk to him already,"* and *"If you don't want to talk, you could just go for a kiss, and you'll have your answer."*

I really wish we could have a sister night right now.

Seamus gives me a knowing look. "Bloke has it bad for ya."

"What? Who?"

It's Friday evening, the last day of our intense week-long research foundations course, and everyone is out celebrating at O'Callahan's. The intensity between me and Finn has escalated throughout the week with no real conversations other than about the research. It's been weird, and I miss him. Even though he's only just come back into my life, being around him changes things. Tomorrow we leave for Brigid's Crossing, where we'll be alone together the majority of the summer. Just the thought sets butterflies fluttering in my stomach.

"No, we're just friends," I tell Seamus, as much for myself as him. "And to be honest, we haven't even really been friends the past few days. We have... issues from before."

Seamus raises an eyebrow.

I'm so ready for this high school drama to be over. We've graduated, and it feels like I'm back in freshman year. "Anyway." I redirect the topic. "Do your aunt and uncle really own Brigid's Crossing?"

"Aye. My ma's sister, Aunt Nora. I spent a lot of time on the farm durin' school and it was grand. Aunt Nora and Uncle Malachy are the only family I have left."

"What about your parents?"

"Both gone. Accident at sea. Ship sank right into Dublin Bay."

"Oh, Seamus, I'm so sorry. Does…"

"Does it bother me workin' on the water every day?"

I nod, a little ashamed my thoughts were so obvious.

"Nah, I spend a lot of my days and evenin's fishin' in the bay. Our crew supplies a large portion of the fish the pub serves. Love bein' on the water. A tribute to them."

I have to say if my heart wasn't already so entangled with another guy, I could really see myself opening up to Seamus. But that's the thing—my heart is with someone else. Someone who is barely talking to me right now. I can't imagine that spending so much time with Seamus tonight will help that very much.

"It was a long time ago, and Aunt Nora and Uncle Malachy are solid. I was lucky to have them."

"I'm looking forward to meeting them even more now."

"Don't let them fool you. They're also ornery as hell."

I laugh as Ryan joins us.

"Teagan, 'tis a beautiful necklace ya've got there." He eyes my emerald.

"Oh, thank you."

Seamus hands Ryan a bar tab. "Ryan's got this thing about emeralds. Crazy about them, if you ask me."

"Me too."

Ryan's grin seems to convey more than just a joined interest. I look away to break the eye contact.

"I better get back with my friends." I push my chair in. "Hopefully I'll see you at the farm one day, Seamus."

"I'll make a point of it."

"The Kavanagh farm?" Ryan's eyes narrow.

"Teagan and Finn are assigned to the farm this summer," Seamus explains.

"Lucky ya." Ryan looks at me a little too long for comfort. His gaze is like a wolf assessing its prey.

The door opens and three men all in black walk toward the bar. The one in front looks our way before settling onto a stool. Turning back to us, he catches my eye, and a coldness runs down my spine. His lips curl up in a devilish grin as his eyes run over me.

Ryan hurries behind the bar to get the men pints.

That's odd. When has anyone in Ireland been in a hurry like that?

"Ya all right?" Seamus studies me.

"Who are those men?"

"Never caught their names, but they come in every few weeks. Some of the folk around here say they're Nathair."

"Nathair?"

"Gaelic for snake. It's the name of a notorious gang up in the north. They lay low for the most part. Never caused any trouble 'round here."

I watch Ryan talking with the men. "I better get back to my friends," I say again, and leave Seamus to serve another round.

"What have you guys been talking about?" Zoey whispers to me.

"Just about our on-site location. Seamus's aunt and uncle are the owners and our mentors for the summer."

"I guess you'll be seeing more of him then."

"Come on, it's not like that. He's a great guy but…"

"You're into someone else."

"Yeah. No. I don't know."

Zoey gives me a sympathetic look. "He's been watching you all night, barely said a word."

"Who? Finn?"

"Teagan, come on! It's so obvious you two are crazy about each other."

"I am not."

She gives me a pointed look and I give in. "OK, I am."

Zoey's smile grows brilliant. "That's the first step—acknowledgement. Now, what is going on with you two?"

"How much time do you have?"

Zoey laughs. "It will all work out."

Before we can really talk, Finn and Kyle come back to the table.

"We should go. We've gotta leave early tomorrow." Finn barely looks at me before heading to the door.

"Hi to you too," I murmur.

As much as I want to argue, he's right. I follow him out the door, anger mounting with each step. We barely make it halfway to the dorm before the last of my willpower crumbles.

"What's your problem?" I snap at him.

He looks taken aback but then scoffs. "Sorry to pull you away from that guy."

"That guy is Seamus, as you very well know. And honestly it's nice to have a friend around here." I walk swiftly by him before turning back around. "Maybe you should be more of a friend. We are partners again, after all. And I never asked Seamus for his number. He gave it to me. He actually said he thinks you... you...never mind. You know, if you have such a problem with him giving it to me, maybe you should say something yourself. Or maybe you should have said something a long time ago. Either way, I'm sick of this unnecessary drama. Grow up!"

I stumble on the last few words, but it feels so good to get it off my chest.

He says nothing for a moment, and when he does, I wish he hadn't. "I don't want to be your friend."

My heart shudders like it's about to break all over again. My stomach churns until I catch the look in his eyes. A look that says things are not over.

He takes a few steps closer. "I've never wanted to *just* be your friend."

My heart pounds so hard I think it might actually leap out of my chest. This is it. After all of this time, I will finally find out how he feels about me now…maybe even how he felt about me then. I've been wishing for this moment for so long that I can barely believe it's happening.

Stopping mere inches away, Finn shakes his head as if clearing the cobwebs. "Listen, I've always cared about you, Teagan, and—"

"There you guys are!"

Kyle's voice breaks the silence as he throws an arm around us. Zoey casts an apologetic look toward me, having sensed what they'd just interrupted.

As if on cue, the rain starts a slow fall, washing away any hope I had of finally knowing how Finn feels. The four of us walk back to the dorm, his unspoken words lost in the night.

Chapter Six

My phone alarm wakes me at 5:30 the next morning. I quickly turn it off, so it doesn't wake Zoey—who's smiling in her sleep. She and Kyle were still up when I finally faded out, a daunting task given my mind was running through every possibility of what could have been.

There's a note on a torn piece of loose leaf on my bag.

Kyle asked me to be his girlfriend! Actually, he asked to "court me," but that's just Kyle. I am so in love!

I have to admit they do seem good for each other, but "in love" seems a bit premature. Her happiness is a thrill for me because I have grown close to both her and Kyle this past week, but it also grates on me a little since I don't seem to be any closer to an answer with Finn.

If he and I had met this week, would it have been love at first sight, like with Kyle and Zoey? Not that I even believe in that, but the thought keeps crossing my mind. Without the confines of high school or a boyfriend I should've never been with, would things have been different for us too?

The familiar tale of my parents falling in love runs through my head like a movie I've seen a hundred times. Deep down I had wondered, and even hoped, I would have a similar story. I mean, who doesn't fantasize about falling in love in the Irish countryside? It's so romantic. *Agh.* I really sound like Kayleigh now. She's the romantic one, not me. I'm the practical one. I make observations and develop theories in an objective, rational way.

That's it—I should be rational about last night. An eighteen-year-old male homo sapien was calculating the appropriate words to profess his undying love for the beautiful and witty eighteen-year-old female.

Ahhh! Okay, I need to stop.

Kayleigh always says that our gut instinct is just as important as any scientific data. I've argued this with her on more than one occasion. And when I say argued, I mean we talked kindly about our opinions. No one can really argue with Kayleigh because she always sees the best in people and tries so hard to understand the other person that you can't get mad, no matter what happens. So, it's really like playing conversational dodgeball with marshmallows.

As if called by my thoughts, my phone rings, and her face appears on the screen. I hurry to answer and slip into the bathroom, hoping to not wake Zoey.

"Kayleigh, so good to hear your voice!"

"Oh, Teagan. Same here. I miss you so much. I just couldn't stop thinking about you and had to try calling, hoping I'd finally catch you.

"Perfect timing, but it's after midnight over there. What are you doing up?"

Kayleigh always likes to be in bed by ten, saying that we can only be our best with the right amount of sleep. I agree on a scientific basis, which leaves Ashling as the night owl in the family. She's often up through the early hours of the morning and is quite grumpy until at least 10 a.m., something that does not bode well for school.

"Okay, let's get right to it. What's going on?"

I fill her in on the week and last night. She listens, like I knew she would, and sighs as deeply as I did when I told her about our lost chance last night.

"Wow. How are you feeling?"

"Honestly, I don't know. So confused. I feel this strong connection with Finn, something I never felt with Scott or anyone else, but I don't know how he feels. I've thought a lot about it, and I can conclude, based on the evidence, that I act differently with Finn. I am more emotional around him than with anyone else. My relationship with Scott was practical and made sense, but it lacked emotion. Around Finn, my emotions seem to go into overdrive. I never would have yelled at Scott like I yelled at Finn last night. I would have talked with Scott, but going into an emotional tornado wouldn't have happened. He and I were together a long time, but if Finn had told me he had feelings for me, I would have broken up with Scott for him."

"You can't go back in time, so don't even think that way. Knowing what you know now, focus on the present and what you want for the future."

"I don't know what I want."

Kayleigh hesitates before asking, "Do you think you're being completely honest with yourself?"

"Have you thought about majoring in counseling or psychology?"

"Yes, actually I have," Kayleigh says brightly. "But you know I want to be a writer. Maybe a minor though. Anyway, now back to you."

I groan. "Do we have to?"

"Yes. I was there during the Finn thing, remember? I have never seen you like that. You were in love, Teagan."

I want to deny it, but she's right. I was head over heels in love with Finn. "I know," I finally admit.

"The only question now is, are you still in love with him?"

The silence stretches.

"Oh, Teagan. This could be a second chance for you guys."

"What if he doesn't want a second chance? What if he never wanted a first chance?"

"I think we both know the answer to that."

My phone beeps with a text from Fiona. "I have to go. Fiona's meeting us downstairs. I'll talk to you soon, okay?"

"Okay," Kayleigh says quietly. "I'll talk to you soon. You know I'm always here."

"I know."

"Love you."

"Love you too."

I end the call, my mind whirling at the realization.

A moment later a text comes through from Kayleigh:

Remember to follow your heart, not just your mind.

I turn off the phone, even though turning it off won't stop the thoughts from coming. With Finn there is a vulnerability that I don't experience with anyone else. The way it hurt me when he left school was so much more than what I should have felt. And I don't want to get hurt again.

I experienced such intense heartache during those classes and lab without him that it was like I had lost the love of my life. April had the right to be heartbroken. They had an actual relationship. Finn and I were just friends, but he said he never wanted to be friends. *No*, he said that he had never wanted to be *just* friends. Isn't it incredible how one word can change something so entirely that it can be the difference between despair and hope?

The smart, logical thing to do would be to stay away from Finn. If I don't open myself up to him again, then I can't get hurt. Cause and effect. If I do one thing, I should expect the other. If I close myself off, then I shouldn't get hurt, right?

I mean, why do I think he was interested in me in high school when he was with April anyway? And April was…well, kind of the opposite of me, actually. I couldn't help but see the difference between the two of us, and if he was interested in her, how could he ever be interested in me? Her short, wavy blond hair to my long, dark, straight hair. She was outgoing and the life of the party, while I have always been quiet and more serious. I was focused on my grades and my goals, while they were always at the parties and happening places.

But there was something between us, even as hard as it was to see them together. I always knew that we would be better together, which wasn't based on any evidence, just a feeling. But feelings aren't trustworthy. Feelings can mislead you and make you see things that aren't there. So, what is true between me and Finn? If only Kyle hadn't come out at just that moment last night, maybe I would know. All the rawness I saw in Finn closed up when they came out. Would he ever open up to me again?

You guys have all summer, just let things happen naturally.

Is Kayleigh right? Maybe I should just let things happen, if they're meant to be. Let everything come about naturally. *Just rip it off like a bandage and talk to him already.* Or maybe Ashling has the right idea. Her way would be quick and painful at first, but I would finally know. No more questions or what ifs. I would have an answer.

Zoey stirs in her sleep, murmuring something about cheeseburgers that makes me laugh. I will miss rooming with Zoey. I can only hope that wherever I end up for college, I will have a roommate as great as her. I write her a quick note on the paper and leave it on her desk.

Last night we promised to keep in touch during the summer. I'll text her after we settle into the farm. Zoey, Kyle, and Maria have been assigned Overlook Point, an old castle in Country Clare. They are staying in a bed and breakfast nearby, and there are tales of it being haunted, which Kyle is psyched for. I wonder how Maria will fit into Kyle and Zoey's already tight bond. It should make for an interesting group. I remind myself that while these are my friends, they're also my competition. I need to stay focused on the ultimate goal.

Fiona is picking us up in fifteen minutes. I packed last night, so there's not much more to do this morning. I make myself focus on getting ready, deciding on my comfiest pair of faded blue jeans and a cream knit hoodie. Warm enough for the crisp morning air, and comfortable for the 60-degree weather later in the day. The forecast is calling for a mostly clear day, so hopefully we will get some time without rain to move in and tour the farm. I leave my hair loose, with gold knot studs glinting from my earlobes. I carefully swipe on some black mascara, peach blush, and pink lip gloss. As I lace up my hikers, I feel ready for whatever today may bring.

~

We arrive at the farm just before eight, after a mostly silent hour-long drive. Fiona wishes us good luck and promises to be in touch soon. Her normally peppy eyes are drooping, with little smudges of mascara under them, and her hair is disheveled. She looks like she had a late night too.

Waving goodbye to Fiona, I look at the old farmhouse before us. Running a hand through my hair, I check the schedule for today. "We're supposed to meet with Malachy Kavanagh," I say aloud, "but there doesn't seem to be any-one around. Think we should go look for him?"

Finn shrugs, looking like he hasn't a care in the world. "Maybe we should just knock on the front door."

The simplicity of his response irks me. Of course I had thought of that, but the itinerary for today says he's meeting us by the front entrance. Only he isn't here.

I shrug back, imitating Finn with exaggerated movement, and his mouth hints at a smile. He knocks with three swift taps.

Nothing.

"Where can they be?" I scan the portfolio in search of a phone number. I'm about to call Fiona when a man's voice sounds through the air.

"Gandalf, you eejit!"

Finn and I exchange a questioning look before following the voice around to a back field. My mouth drops at the sight of an older man covered head to toe with mud, holding a sticky lead rope and pointing a finger at the grey horse in front of him. At least I think it was grey before the apparent mud bath.

"Malachy, what on earth are ya doin' out there? Can't ya just leave well enough alone?" A plump older woman rushes out the back door swinging a tattered dish towel in her hand. "Ye're a fright to be seen!"

My boots sink slowly into the soft ground, but the woman is light on her feet, not at all fazed by the soggy ground as she moves flawlessly toward the gate.

"Don't think ye're coming into this house covered in that mess," she hollers over the gate.

Out of the corner of my eye, I see Finn's lips twitch.

The man doesn't answer, but darts to the side again as the horse runs by, sending more mud into the air.

The quirk on Finn's lips is a full-blown grin now as he leans against the large willow tree. Catching my eye, he sends a wink like we're in on this secret together.

"Eejit!" The woman calls before turning back to the house.

"Excuse me," I say as politely and professionally as I can. "I'm Teagan and this is Finn. We're here with the Emerald Isle Summer Scholars program. We're scheduled to meet with Malachy Kavanagh, the farm manager."

The woman finally notices us, and a large smile grows on her weathered face. The laugh lines around her eyes suggest a woman who has had a lot to be cheerful about in her life. "Good day!" She sweeps an arm towards the man. "Malachy will be in in a bit, unless that horse finally puts him in an early grave. Both too stubborn to see straight."

We follow her into the old farmhouse as a whinnying sound rises from the field.

Walking into the house is like coming home. Like sliding into a comfortable chair, familiar and cozy.

"Ya two go on and have a seat in the sittin' room. I'll be right in with some tea."

Finn and I sit on the small sofa, leaving the two recliners for Mr. and Mrs. Kavanagh. It's a small room but open, with white walls and natural light. A wood fireplace sits center on the main wall, with an oak mantle housing framed family photos. One of those catches my eye.

"It's Seamus." I smile as I pick up the framed photo of a boy, no older than ten, dark messy hair and deep brown, somewhat ornery eyes. An undeniable resemblance to Seamus. Dirt streaks his cheeks, and the dimple from his glowing smile says he couldn't be happier.

"Right ya are. I take it ya've met our nephew?" Mrs. Kavanagh places the tea tray on a small buffet in the corner, pulling out four white teacups and saucers.

"We all met at O'Callahan's in Dublin."

"Works too hard he does. I keep tellin' him that, but the bugger was never one to listen." She wipes her hands on her apron and joins me at the mantle. "But always a good heart."

"It seems like you two are close. He told me he had the best time here at the farm."

"Aye. Poor lad had a hard time of it when his parents passed— God rest their souls. He doesn't often come these days. Always so busy with the pub or the boat." She gives a shake of her head before returning to the tea tray.

"Can I help you, Mrs. Kavanagh?" I reach to help sturdy the tea tray.

"Ah, call me Nora. And Malachy is just fine for the old grump. Now, ya have a seat and I'll bring this right over."

As I resume my spot by Finn, he gives me a weak smile. "I didn't know Seamus's parents died or that he's related to the Kavanaghs."

"Well, you wouldn't join us last night, so I bet there's a lot you don't know."

I flinch at the briskness of my words.

"I didn't want to interrupt," he fires back.

"There was—there is nothing to interrupt. Which you would know very well if you would take the time to talk to me."

"I tried last night, but—"

"Ah, a nice warm cup o' black tea is just what we need." Nora hands a cup to each of us, a questioning look in her eyes.

I can't believe we were just about to have this conversation here, right in front of our research mentor. What am I thinking?

"Isn't it grand?"

"Yes, thank you, Nora." I make myself sound professional again.

"It's great." Finn sounds completely at ease, except for the slight edge to his tone.

Nora looks back and forth between us, no doubt trying to puzzle out the situation. Before she can ask any questions, the back door opens and Malachy stomps into the house.

"Boots!" Nora exclaims, narrowing her eyes at the trail of mud in his wake.

"Ah." He steps outside for a moment, then returns in just his wool socks, a big toe sticking out of the right one.

"That devil in horse clothes has lost his mind! Tommy's out there tryin' to clean the buggar off." He slides into a recliner without so much as a nod in our direction.

"That's makes two of ye then." Nora hands him a cup of tea. "But enough of that horse. We have company."

Malachy finally sees us, and a grin lights his face. "Ah, *cead mile failte!*"

"I'm Finn and this is Teagan. We're with the Emerald Isle summer program."

"Right ye are!" Malachy gets up and sticks out his hand, shaking each of ours with a firm and slightly too-spirited grip. "I didn't know ye'd be here today!"

This is not looking good for our mentorship.

"Malachy, come on now. These two are goin' think ye're mad if you continue this way." Nora swipes at him with her towel before turning to us. "It's just grand having ye here."

"Malachy, I have Gandalf in the stall. I'm gonna work on that fence," a man calls from the kitchen.

"Wait just a minute, Tommy. A cup o' tea first."

"No thanks, Nora. I'm fine."

"Tommy is from America too—Virginia." Malachy draws out the word.

"Oh, so close. We're from Maryland," I tell him. Immediately I'm reminded of the conversation with Finn. Does he say he's from Maryland or one of the other places he's lived?

A tall man who looks to be in his early twenties joins us from the kitchen. Light, curly brown hair frames a strong nose and dark eyes. Dressed all in black, he looks like he could be in a rock band.

"Teagan and Finn are with Emerald Isle and will be here for the summer," Nora explains.

A flash of hesitation crosses Tommy's face. "It will be nice seeing you around." He nods at us before walking out the back door.

"He's a wee bit shy. Had a hard time of it growin' up in that home of his," Nora tells us.

"A fine good worker. Took to the horses in no time," Malachy says, pride in his voice.

"He was lookin' for work in Dublin when Malachy came across him." Nora leans forward. "In a bad state he was."

"Offered him a job right then and there. Know a good man when I see one."

Nora reaches over and squeezes his hand. "That ya do. And so do I for that matter."

In that moment, I see that despite the bickering, their love is true. Averting my gaze from the private moment, I see a rustic, woven St. Brigid's cross above the door frame.

"St. Brigid herself used to cross this very land," Malachy says.

Finn puts his cup down. "That amazing. Are there any stories about her in the area?"

"Too many to count." Nora sighs. "We'll get to those. All in good time. Teagan, I'll show ya to yer room upstairs, while Malachy acquaints Finn to the cottage."

"You'll be sharin' the cottage with Tommy," Malachy tells Finn. "Separate rooms, and as we said, Tommy keeps to himself."

"Thank you." Finn and I speak in unison, while walking in separate directions.

Once upstairs, I study my small bedroom. White lace curtains, tied back with ribbons, allow sunbeams to highlight the pale-yellow angles of the walls. A single bed covered with a white quilt sits in a cubby between two sloping walls. Running my fingers over the embroidered flowers stitched on the quilt, I study the painting hanging above the bed. A vibrant landscape of deep blues, greens, oranges, and yellows draws me in. The paint is applied in such a way as to give it a three-dimensional appearance. Something feels familiar about it, like from a dream.

"Ow." I stumble as my shin hits the leg of the writing desk in the corner. Made of oak, it has a vintage look with its tiny drawers and intricate carvings. A shamrock paperweight sits on top of a stack of writing paper, with a fountain pen laid next to it. As I envision myself sitting here and writing home, a warmth bubbles up inside me.

I pull out the drawers of the matching dresser and empty my suitcase for the first time since arriving in Ireland. I pause when my hand brushes something at the bottom of my bag.

The journal. I haven't written in it once. Uncapping the fountain pen, it's weight heavy in my hand, I open to the first page.

Smoothing the binding I write, *I'm here.*

For now, that's all that comes out.

Chapter Seven

"The past couple days have flown by. The Kavanaghs have been so warm and welcoming that it feels like I've known them forever. They're one of those old married couples who are practically one," I tell Kayleigh. "They are a team that has been working together for so long that one doesn't seem to exist without the other."

I pause and wonder if I will ever find that kind of love, the kind that only grows stronger with time.

"Oh, that's so sweet," Kayleigh responds. "I can't wait to meet them. I just wish I didn't have to wait until the end of the program to visit."

"It will be nice to have you guys here." But my emotions are a bit conflicted, because if they're here then the program is at an end. And I'm not even close to being ready for that.

"So, how are things with Finn?"

I curl into my pillows. "I have no idea. I keep catching him watching me and it seems like he's trying to figure me out or something. We haven't talked about *us* since that night before coming here."

Kayleigh murmurs in sympathy.

I groan into the pillow. "This isn't what was supposed to happen this summer. I didn't plan for any of this, and yet it's happening, and there are times when I look at Finn and can't believe my good luck in being here with him. And then there are times when I feel cursed because it's shaken my plans to the core. It's like my mind and heart are playing a game of tug-of-war and I don't know which side to cheer for."

"It's life, Teagan. There will always be choices. You need to go with your instincts."

"My heart, you mean."

"Well, I think listening to your heart could be best in this case."

"Maybe. I wish Finn and I would at least agree on a research topic. I've been planning to study the best chemical soil concentrations for crop growth and creating our own fertilizer. Things that would be perfect for all the farms. But Finn's idea is more about sustainable energy—green energy. We haven't been able to find common ground yet."

"Maybe you two need to find something completely yours. Like instead of what you've been planning on for years, compromise on a topic that interests you both."

Leave it to Kayleigh to see the best in the situation.

"I think you're right. It's just strange being here, you know? Being on the farm helps though."

"I bet it does. I know the horses are missing you at home."

"I miss them too. I miss all of you. I'll call you again soon."

"Okay. Love you, Teagan. Enjoy every moment!"

"I will. Love you too."

I disconnect, then roll over and cover my head with a pillow. Kayleigh's right. I should be enjoying every moment.

The bending and creaking of each step as I walk downstairs is starting to sound familiar. I enter the sitting room to see Malachy reclining in his chair, his reading glasses shielding eyes that are closed.

"Teagan?" He barely moves his mouth.

"Oh, I hope I didn't wake you. I was just wondering if I could groom one of the horses?"

"Just resting my eyes. Does a wonder of good." He rubs his eyes. "Ya can groom 'em whenever ye'd like. Shannon is with 'em now."

"Shannon?"

"Wee one from the town. Sweet as pie but cursed by lameness. Sad sight it is. Comes with her ma to visit Nora and they always stay with the horses. She loves 'em, she does."

"I'm sure she does."

His eyes drift close and I try to make a quiet exit.

By the time I reach the stable, I can already feel my stress and confusion melting away. There's something therapeutic in just being around the horses.

Gandalf snorts in the far-left stall. I stifle the urge to walk over to him. Instead, I choose Sam, the large Irish Draught, mostly because he will take more time than the others to groom. Standing at 16.1 hands high, he is a brilliant grullo in color. It's rare to see a horse in the blue roan shade, and it gives him a feel of majesty. Sam, in all his wonder, stands loyally by my side awaiting our next move. An apt name indeed. Actually, all of the horse's names are perfectly matched. It brings warmth to my heart seeing how the Kavanaghs really understand their horses and their unique personalities.

I laugh as I think about when Finn and I met the horses for the first time. Finn was so excited upon seeing the names and their connection to Lord of the Rings. He and Malachy talked for so long about the LOTR stories that Nora and I left to make dinner.

I lead Sam to the cross ties, and he stands majestically. His calm demeanor is like a medicine to my frazzled nerves. Horses are known to reflect emotions, like a mirror to the soul. My parents always taught us that the horses instinctively read our emotions and respond accordingly. I've found it to be true over the years, and looking at Sam now, I wonder if horses can also promote change to our emotional states.

I fit the curry comb over my palm and begin a rhythmic circling over his back. His eyes droop and my mind wanders to an article my parents were discussing not long before I left. I remember it like it was yesterday. They were seated at the small kitchen window seat, leaning over their coffees with one of the science journals that always takes up residence on our kitchen counter. When I was younger, the articles were too difficult to read by myself and I would re-read the abstracts and summaries over and over until either my mom or dad found me and would read the whole article to me, stopping to explain what was happening in a way that I could understand.

A small wave of homesickness flows over me. Thinking about those moments makes me long to be back in the comfort and safety of my home, but as soon as it comes, the longing begins to recede.

"Being here," I murmur to Sam, "I don't know how to explain it, but it feels right. Like something was missing before."

He nuzzles my shoulder.

"You understand, don't you, boy?" Moving to the other side, I continue brushing out the loose hair as I consider my place here. "I am here for a reason. I feel that so strongly."

Sam leans towards me.

Still, there is a haze of uncertainty about my actual purpose. I have always been so focused on my goals and the steps to get there, that now I feel a little bit lost, actually being here, even though I'm following my plan with precision. That's not supposed to happen. The research ideas Finn and I discussed just feel…off. As hard as it is to admit, Kayleigh is right—it's time to let go of our pre-conceived ideas and come up with something that's ours.

"I see love everywhere I look these days," I tell Sam. "Like those two." I nod to Aragorn and Arwen who are nuzzling each other through a cutaway section of their stalls. They really are the most adorable horses. While I've seen bonded horses before, none have been quite as affectionate as these two bays. Just seeing them sends my mind back to thoughts of love and a special someone.

A squeal of laughter rings from the stable entrance and a young girl approaches. She's maybe seven or eight, her arms secured with metal walking canes. As she walks, her knees cross in a scissor-like movement and her resemblance to little Abby is uncanny. A smile grows on her round face, where a splash of freckles scatter over her nose. Long, strawberry blonde hair is tied neatly in two braids, pink ribbons at the end. Bright blue eyes are locked on Sam.

"She loves the horses." A woman with the same blonde hair and blue eyes stands behind her. She guides Shannon with a gentle hand on her back. "Never see her as happy as here. Her heart is strong. If only her body would follow."

Her eyes take on a wishful look before sadness takes over.

"Cerebral palsy?" I ask softly.

"It is." She grimaces before stretching out a hand. "I'm Brianna, and this is my daughter, Shannon."

"Teagan." I shake her hand. "I'm staying with the Kavanaghs for the summer."

"Aye, the research students. How excitin'."

"Yeah. We're loving it here."

"M-m-m-m-a!" Shannon squeals, a distinct shakiness to her voice.

Brianna helps her daughter reach Sam, her thin arms stretched wide to embrace him. Giggles explode from her delicate mouth, and I feel a familiar warmness, one that sets memories of home swirling in my mind.

"Has she ever ridden Sam?" I ask, an idea already forming.

"Oh, nah. Never."

"Have you ever heard of equine-assisted therapy?" At her blank look, I take a deep breath and continue. "It's not just horseback riding, but a range of exercises and movements that help promote muscle strength, balance, and stability. It helps so many people with all kinds of disabilities, and cerebral palsy is one of them."

"Nothin' like that out here I'm afraid. My guess is it's not somethin' we'd ever be able to afford neither."

"If the cost wasn't an issue, would you be open to letting Shannon ride on Sam?" I ask, excitement lacing every word. "Of course, it would be with the proper restraints and gear."

"I'm not sure. I really can't afford it."

"Honestly, there would be no cost at all. I'll take care of it all. I could work with her. Nothing official or anything, just for fun and exercise. My family has a horse farm back in the US and my mom works with equine therapy. Shannon is so much like Abby, a little girl in her program. She has cerebral palsy too and has made so much improvement since beginning sessions with Mom. I think Shannon could too."

Hope sparkles in Brianna's eyes once again. "Well, that would be very kind of you. I'd have to pay you somethin'…I make a good pot pie."

"That would be perfect."

I help Shannon use the curry comb and Sam begins chewing, a sure sign of contentment.

This is going to work.

When they leave a few minutes later, after promising to come back in a couple days, Shannon's legs are shaking from the time spent standing, but her smile is bright, contentment covering her face.

"That was incredible."

Finn's standing at the stable entrance, hands in the pockets of his jeans.

"Yeah." I give Sam a quick kiss on his nose. "It never ceases to amaze me."

I take a deep breath, building up the courage to plead my case. "This is what our research should be."

Finn raises an eyebrow.

Okay, well, that wasn't the most eloquent way to say it.

"Equine-assisted activities. I propose we study the effects of equine-assisted activities on people with special needs."

Finn takes a moment to consider the proposal, looking a bit skeptical but intrigued. "I like the idea, but don't know a lot about equine-assisted activities."

"Not long ago, my parents came home from a conference all excited about possibly starting something new at the farm. They learned about equine-assisted activities and therapeutic riding from a workshop. They've always been so invested in the rescue that this area never really came into focus until recently. And I was so busy with graduation stuff, that I didn't pay too much attention, but I remember seeing them outside, working with the horses." I feel my excitement rising. "See, it's all connected to the human-animal bond. Based on neurology and biophysics, how our brain communicates with our body and the effect a horse has on those connections. You saw Shannon and Sam. They have a connection."

"Yeah. Like Malachy and Gandalf." Finn laughs.

"You're kidding?"

"Come on, you've had to have seen them. They are so in tune to each other."

Finn's right. In all of Malachy's grumpiness toward the horse, I missed it. "How did I not see it before? It's not just physical connection, it's emotional too."

I pull out my phone and type a quick text. "Hopefully my parents can send the research they have or the contact for the person from the conference and we can get started with our proposal." Then I remember that Finn hasn't actually agreed to the topic. "If that's okay with you."

"I think it's perfect. Let's start planning after tea with the Kavanaghs."

"Sounds like a plan." The relief of those words is doing wonders for the tension in my shoulders. My gaze stops on the St. Brigid's cross hanging above the stable door. "It's all coming together."

Sam startles at the sound of a metal bucket crashing to the floor.

"Oh, I'm sorry. Didn't know anyone was still here." Tommy comes out of the tack room. And points to the cross. "They're all over the farm. Seems you can't look anywhere without seeing one. But this one is special. Kinda draws your eye, you know?"

Tommy runs a hand down Sam's neck, and Sam returns the gesture as he snorts into Tommy's shoulder. "Hey, big boy."

"Yeah." I can feel the draw too. "This cross looks bigger than others I've seen."

Tommy looks up at the cross again while Sam eats a peppermint from his hand. "I think it was special to Malachy's dad. He once told me that his dad would point to it and say, 'To give all you have to help another is where you'll find true treasure.' Said it so many times, it's hard to forget."

He shakes his head and returns to the tack room.

"Sam, looks like our time is up." I kiss the horse's cheek and secure his stall door before walking with Finn to the house. The first spark of hope for our research since we arrived has been ignited.

～

We sit around the table sipping tea for a few minutes before Finn broaches the subject. "We have an idea for our research proposal," Finn explains, "and we're hoping for your help."

The Kavanaghs nod at us, concern edging their features. "This is our first time doin' the program. I hope we can help." Unease is clear in her voice.

"You are already helping so much," I tell her. "We'd like to start an equine-assisted activities program, focusing on equine-assisted therapy. We would love to use the farm as the base for the program, if that would be okay with you guys."

She smiles at this, but it doesn't quite reach her eyes. "'Tis a wonderful farm, but I'm not sure how it would work."

"We would set it all up," I say quickly. "We actually got the idea watching Shannon and Sam together. We think the program could help a lot of people considering there's nothing like it in the area."

After explaining my personal experience at home, Malachy and Nora look interested.

"And ya think we could do that here?" Nora asks.

"Yes," Finn and I say together. Our eyes lock and for the first time in days, it feels like we're partners again.

"Indeed." Malachy nods. "The thing is the farm …" He drifts off, lost in thought.

After a few moments, Finn clears his throat. "Could you tell us a little more about the farm?"

Malachy seems to relax with his question.

"Ah, it was rare ol' times." Malachy leans forward, elbows on his knees in what I've come to recognize as his storytelling position. "The farm has been in my family for generations."

"I think we need to start with St. Brigid herself." Nora speaks as if her and St. Brigid share an intimate friendship.

"Right ya are. St. Brigid was born around the year 453 to a slave mother, Brocca, and a pagan chieftain father, Dubhthach. When Dubthach's wife found out Brocca was pregnant, she sold her to a Druid landowner. Brigid grew up to be very generous, givin' away everythin' she could find to the poor, even though she was quite poor herself. There's talk of her and her ma knowin' St. Patrick himself."

"Baptized by him too." Nora adds sugar to her tea.

"Aye. When she reached ten years of age, Brigid was returned to her father's home, since he was her legal master. Her generosity continued, her givin' away anythin' she could to those who asked."

"Puttin' her father in quite the temper."

"Right ya are. He goes to the King of Ireland himself to sell her, but the king sets her free instead. Must have been a scene to behold!"

"She went back to live with her ma and the Druid. She gave away much milk, but the milk never depleted. Miracles. Dubthach eventually came around, as most men do." Nora winks at us. "And eventually agreed to allow Brigid to enter the convent and even gave her money to start her very own monastery."

"The first of many."

"She was the abbess of the monastery right here in Kildare. T'was a center for learnin'. Art, metal work, and beautifully illustrated scriptures."

"Some of the student's illustrations are right down the street at St. Patrick's. Be worth the visit to see 'em."

"I'd love to see them." My heart leaps at the thought.

"Me too." Finn's eye shine with excitement. There's the passion that has always drawn me to him.

"We'll make an outin' of it!" Nora beams, swirling her tea.

Malachy seems oblivious to our side conversation and continues like nothing was said. "Da would always fuss over those ancient farrier tools. No good to use, mind ya. The legend is they were crafted in the monastery and were used by St. Brigid herself. Da never let us near 'em, but Ma took me to see them one day. The metal heavy in my hands, I thought I was on the top o' the world."

"A treasure, if only we knew where Eamon hid them. He was always hidin' things."

"Speaking of treasure," Finn says carefully. "We heard a story about a lost emerald on a farm in Kildare."

"Ah, the emerald!" Malachy gleams. "Right here on this very land. Fifty some years ago my Da was in New York City for a business meetin'. Important horse breeder he was. While there, he met a Columbian man by the name of Enrique Diaz. He and his family were escapin' trials in their homeland. Ma always said Da took one look at their daughter, her big brown eyes shinin', and offered Enrique a job right there on the spot. They traveled back with him to Ireland, much to Ma's surprise. Ma and Darlisa grew close and Luciana and I were inseparable. Ma loved havin' Luciana around, helpin' with her garden. Enrique and Da worked seamlessly together, breeding those horses. He was a natural horseman, Da always said."

His eyes take on a weary look and Nora continues for him.

"Five years passed, and then the Diaz family decided it was time for them to return home."

"Oh, that must have been so hard." I imagine the loss that must have caused Malachy's family.

"Indeed." Nora got a faraway look in her eyes. "Broke Eamon and Roisin's hearts. I remember when news spread that they were leavin' town, my own Ma cried at our kitchen table. They were a part of Cloverdale, and everyone was sorry to see 'em go."

"Aye. It was a hard time," Malachy agreed. "Luciana cried her little heart out." By the look on Malachy's face, he'd had a hard time letting go too.

"See, they had become family. That's how it is here." Nora settles her head back on the chair.

"But they had their family in Columbia too, don't forget. Darlisa's father was ill, and they needed to go home to be with him."

"Malachy had a whole box of letters Luciana sent him, but they were lost in a stable fire a few years back." Nora squeezes Malachy's hand.

"Shouldn't've ever put them in that barn, but Da thought that was the safest place when I was a lad. We built it back up and I will never let another fire take it down again."

Seeing Malachy today, it seems as though he also finds comfort in the stable.

"Then the rumors of the emerald began swirlin' 'round town," Nora explains. "Talk was Eamon had lost his mind in superstition and thought it would bring bad luck if he kept the family emerald. So, word spread that he buried it somewhere on this very land."

Finn and I look to Malachy.

"Ma saw him drawing the map. But we never spoke of it again. To this day I haven't the slightest idea if any of it is true."

"Do you believe it?" I ask Nora.

"I don't *not* believe it." Her mouth curves up and her eyes seem to twinkle. "I'm a woman of faith, and I believe this farm is blessed, emerald or not."

My affection for these two grows by the day. Malachy and Nora are exceptional people, and I'm beginning to think there's a reason I'm here on this farm with them. I feel almost as if God has called me here, and placed them in my life for a purpose.

"Shortly after we were married," Nora says, "Malachy's folks passed from a rough bout of the flu. Dreaded curse."

"That's right. Before Ma passed she pulled us close and told us straight out that Da did bury that emerald, and there's indeed a map, but she didn't have the slightest idea of where to find either of them."

"The farm was in a bit of disarray then." Nora patted Malachy's hand. "Needed money to fix it up, but none to be found. Luck would have it, we secured a loan from the bank."

"Wouldn't have happened without Mac." Malachy holds a hand up, and they cross themselves.

"Mac, or John McGarvey," Nora explains, "is an ol' friend of Malachy's. Helped us with a loan when we thought it would never come."

"Possessor of unusual business abilities, he is." Malachy laughs. "A born wit, but an even truer friend. Never knew a better man."

"The farm became ours, and we kept the promise to Ma to bring it back to its glory. We started hirin' people that needed work and a second chance and, rememberin' the cross held in her hands right till the end, *Brigid's Crossing* seemed a grand name. Though, I fear we may again need help. The farm is more than a bit behind on bills. The money has been disappearin' like coins in ol' Charlie's hand at the pub."

"Farm expenses are risin'."

"Could someone be taking the money?" Finn asks cautiously.

"Never!" They deny together. "We're family here."

"Now see, we lost our wee ones before birth." Nora sends a teary smile to Malachy. "They were too dear for this world. And one day, by the grace of Our Lord, we will be with them again."

"*Mo cara.*" Malachy squeezes his wife's hand. "Others are given to our care in the world."

"Indeed. Everyone we employ and all of the animals are rescues. Seen as hopeless cases to the world, but not in our eyes."

"By doin' good by them, we are followin' the Lord's call for us."

"If only we knew where Da buried that emerald, all our problems would be solved."

Glass shatters in the kitchen.

"Tommy?" Nora hurries to the kitchen entryway.

"Sorry, Nora. Glass slipped right outta my hand." Beads of sweat shine from his forehead, a contrast to the cool draft whiffing through the house.

"Let me help ya, lad." She puts an arm around Tommy and leads him out of the room.

"Sorry to cut this short, but Tommy has these episodes," Malachy says before following her into the side room.

A stillness fills the room with their exit.

"That was odd," Finn remarks.

"It was…I need some air."

I walk out the kitchen door and breathe in the fresh air, trying to figure out what just happened.

Chapter Eight

My mind is still full of the Kavanaghs' story when Finn joins me on the wooden swing by the stable. Without a word, he slides in beside me.

"Crazy day, huh?"

"Yeah. I need time to absorb it all, you know?"

"Absolutely."

We swing for a couple minutes before I turn to him. "Finn, can I ask you something?"

Understanding fills his eyes as he leans towards me, like he already knows the question I'm about to ask. He nods slowly.

This is my chance to finally ask the question that has plagued my mind almost every moment since we met.

"Did you ever…" I take a deep breath, trying to pull every ounce of courage, "have…feelings for me? I mean, a long time ago, you know, back in school."

I finally said it. A mixture of relief and apprehension immediately washes over me.

His gaze drifts to the ground, expression unreadable. Warmth burns my cheeks as the silence stretches a bit too long. I begin to slide from the swing, but his hand stops me.

"Yeah."

"Me too," I say before I can stop myself.

"Only," his mouth begins to arch in that adorable smile I fell for back in those chemistry labs, "it wasn't just back in school."

My heart trips at his words.

"Teagan, I've liked you since the first day we met. I saw you and knew…you were different. As we spent more time together, I…fell more and more…" He breaks off and runs a hand through his hair.

My eyes burn with the realization of his words. I was right! There's always been something special between us.

"I didn't tell you back then because I couldn't." His eyes cloud and there's pain in the haze. "Even though you were with Scott, I thought in time we would get together. But it was just too hard. I was getting in too deep and needed to put some space between us, so I started dating April. I know it wasn't right to lead her on, but I desperately needed a distraction. Although, I soon realized there's no distracting me from you."

"I wanted to say something. I should have, but… I should've never been with Scott. We were friends for so long and it seemed like we should be together, but we weren't good together. Not really. I don't know why I stayed with him for so long. And then you were with April, and I thought—"

"I shouldn't have been with April either. I was just trying to get over you."

We shake our heads at the ridiculousness of the situation.

"I wish I had said something then, but we're here now and I'm not going to make the same mistake again."

He takes my hands in his, rubs his thumb over my palm, and looks at our united hands as if they hold the answers to the questions that linger between us. Maybe they do. Maybe our hands fit together the same way that our hearts do, only one can be seen and the other only felt.

"Teagan, want to try this again? Just us this time. Since we met, no one else could ever get to me like you do. I don't see how anyone else could." His deep caramel eyes, so soft and gentle in this moment, look into mine, searching. "You wanna give us a chance?"

"Yes."

The word comes out more like a heartfelt prayer than an answer. This is the answer to so many prayers I've prayed over the years. The realization that it's finally happening hits me. "Yes, yes, yes!" I laugh, the giddiness overcoming the remainder of my nerves.

He kisses me for the first time, and the world spins like we're the only two people in the universe. Nothing else matters except what's happening right here, right now. The past is the past for a reason. The future is unknown. But this—this moment is real.

When we finally part, Malachy and Nora are smiling at us through the kitchen window.

Finn laughs, nodding in their direction. "I think we have an audience."

"I don't even care."

We kiss again, then go back inside to get ready for our day in Dublin tomorrow.

~

The city looks different this time, as if I'm seeing an old friend rather than experiencing the nervous excitement of a first date. It's raining, but the rain barely fazes me anymore. I've grown accustomed to the constant dampness and fog. It only makes me further appreciate the rare appearance of the sun.

As we turn onto the university campus, the historic stone greets us with the elegance of hundreds of years of curious minds and daring dreamers. It seems like a lifetime since we were in this place. This time Finn and I are an official couple. Just thinking about the uncertainty and questions that plagued me last time we were here sends a wave of nervous energy through me. Seeming to sense this, Finn reaches over and squeezes my hand. We're in this together and somehow that changes everything.

"Teagan! Finn!" Zoey calls to us from down the main hallway. She drops Kyle's hand and runs to me, wrapping me in a big hug.

"Wait, what's going on here?" She points her finger between the two of us. "Are you guys…?"

I nod with what I'm sure is the biggest smile ever recorded, and Zoey lets out a screech as she jumps up and down.

"What going on?" Kyle asks.

"They're finally together!" Zoey claps her hands in pure excitement.

"Who? These two? No way. Never thought that'd happened." His feigned surprise has us all laughing.

"Was it that obvious?" I'm still a little giddy with the newness of this actually being real and not one of my many high school daydreams.

"Yeah." They speak in unison as Finn catches my eye and we both laugh.

Seriously, why did it take us so long to get here?

"Looks like we have a lot of catching up to do tonight." Zoey winks.

"My thoughts exactly."

Finn and I make it to our meeting with Fiona just in time. She welcomes us into her office, and we take the two chairs opposite her desk.

"So, how're things goin' for ya two?"

Finn and I smile at each other. "Great," he says, taking my hand.

Fiona raises an eyebrow. "Right. To clarify, how's ye're research goin'?"

"Honestly, amazing." It's the absolute truth, even though Fiona looks a bit bored. "It's been really interesting so far, and there's so much history and folklore at the farm."

Fiona's eyes brighten at this. "Is that so? Find anythin' of interest?"

"The Kavanaghs told us more about the lost emerald."

Fiona straightens in her seat.

"But don't worry, we're focusing on the project. The emerald is just an interesting story."

Fiona eyes me closely before her smile returns. "Well, everyone needs a bit of fun."

And on that note we review the parameters of the research and brainstorm ideas together. I'm so thankful Fiona is our mentor. Not everyone would be as supportive as her.

~

Later that evening, we find an open table in the pub and settle in for a night of catching up with Zoey and Kyle. There's a relaxed feeling as we order, and suddenly I feel like high school was a million years ago, and not the few weeks since graduation. Can time really change so quickly? Looking at Finn, I know the answer. Yes, it absolutely can.

We talk about our research assignments, and they get a kick out of the Kavanaghs, especially Malachy and Gandalf.

"They sound like a blast," Zoey says.

"Our mentor's great and the castle is freaking awesome," Kyle says, leaning in closer, "but Maria is starting to look like she's ready to kill us."

"I think she's feeling like a third wheel or something, which is ridiculous. And she's not trying to hide it at all." Zoey gives me a knowing look.

I can imagine Maria being the odd one out in their group. While I don't know her well, I don't see her as one to take being the outsider easily.

"Hopefully things will get better." I try to keep things positive.

As if our conversation beckons her, Maria comes through the pub doors looking absolutely amazing in a form-fitting red dress with matching lipstick. Her white leather ankle boots click on the wooden floor. A matching leather handbag hangs from her wrist on a gold chain. Her long black hair is curled, and she looks more like she stepped off the runway than out of the dorm room, while my white jeans and black-smocked shirt make me look very much like the student I am. Although I bet even in my outfit, Maria could never look like a student. She has a cosmopolitan vibe that I could never pull off, which is fine with me because I am comfortable with who I am. And the greatest guy in the world seems to think I'm pretty darn amazing too.

At this thought I turn toward Finn, drink in his gorgeous profile, and reach for his hand under the table. His smile is all I need to know that he's as happy as I am right now.

"It's so nice to go out again." Maria sighs dramatically as she pulls a chair to the other side of Finn.

I meet Zoey's eyes and I know we're thinking the same thing—Maria is on a mission. I can almost feel the energy radiating off her.

"I'm getting a drink." She gets up and struts to the bar. Seriously, struts. How does she do it? Like everyone else, I can't help but watch.

She's overtly flirting with Seamus, but surprisingly he doesn't act any different with her than he does with any of us. He hands her a pint with a smile, but quickly turns to get the next pint to an older gentleman, giving him the same smile. The look on Maria's face is enough to cause the guy approaching her to return to his seat. Maria flips her hair and saunters back with renewed vigor, pushing in closer to Finn.

A few minutes later, Seamus brings our food over and pulls up a chair next to me. Maria's expression is utter bewilderment.

"Malachy and Nora driving you gag yet?"

"No, they're great." I laugh at his expression. "Malachy is quite a character though."

"Aye. No truer words." His gaze lands on my emerald necklace. "He spin the tale of the lost emerald yet?"

"Yeah, it's incredible. What do you think?"

"A good ol' Irish tale."

"You don't believe it?"

"I've never known Nora to utter an untrue word." Seamus shrugs, an unmistakable glint in his eyes.

"What tale is this?" Maria asks, pushing the menu aside.

"Uncle Malachy believes there's a priceless emerald buried somewhere on his farm. Gift of a Colombian farmhand years past. Said to have the power to make ye deepest dreams come true."

Finn and I exchange a glance. The Kavanaghs never mentioned anything about dreams.

"You do believe it?" Maria raises her perfectly shaped eyebrows.

"I'm an Irishman, right?" he asks with a turn of his lips, before heading back to the bar.

"What a *perdente*." Maria rolls her eyes. When we all just look at her, she continues. "You know, a loser."

"You didn't seem to think so a few minutes ago when you were all over him at the bar," Zoey murmurs.

If looks could kill, Maria would be an assassin.

I don't think this conversation is helping with the tension in their group right now, but something in her dismissive attitude riles me too. "He's not a loser. Seamus is a really great guy." I try my best to put Maria in her place while maintaining the peace, but I think I've added gas to the fire.

Maria glares at me. "Of course, you wouldn't think so. You two have been all over each other since the first night."

"Are you serious?"

She twists her red lips in a sneer. "I bet you still have his number, don't you?" Her cat eyes glare at me, intent and watchful, ready to pounce.

"So, what if I do?" I say at the same time Finn says, "Of course she doesn't."

She looks like she just caught an unexpecting mouse, and pointedly looks at Finn. He's staring at me in disbelief, hurt in his eyes. He can't really still be mad about Seamus's number, can he?

"Why wouldn't Teagan keep Seamus's number?" Zoey asks, catching on to the mounting tension. "We're new in the city, and he can help us. It would be foolish not to keep it."

I give Zoey a small smile of gratitude for trying to come to my rescue.

"Is that why you kept his number, Teagan? To help us in this big, scary city?" Maria asks, nonchalantly running her hand up and down Finn's arm, condescension dripping with each word.

My last bit of resolve to maintain any peace is thrown out the window. "No, Maria, that's not why I kept Seamus's number."

Her eyebrows arch, ready to pounce.

Why hasn't Finn moved away from her?

"I knew you were hot for him." She rolls her eyes. "Falling for the bartender. How much more cliché can you get?"

"I do like him," I say more loudly than I intend. "Seamus is a great guy and it's none of your business whose number I keep."

She gives a sneaky laugh. "I need another drink. I'll be sure to let Seamus know you think he's such a great guy." Winking, she walks away, purring like a cat with a mouse in its teeth.

"She's crazy," I murmur to Finn, but he looks away, jaw clenched.

"Okay, wanna head back?" Zoey asks, hope in her voice but a strained expression on her face. "I've been looking forward to that girl's night, Teag."

As we follow Zoey to the door, I catch a glance of Fiona and Ryan in a heated discussion in the corner. She throws up her hands and pushes into the back room, Ryan right behind her.

Looks like she's having a rough night too.

Once outside, I pull Finn toward the park across the street. "We'll see you guys back at the dorm in a few," I call to Zoey and Kyle.

"Okay, what's going on? You're not really upset about Seamus, are you?" I ask Finn when we're alone.

He sighs and pulls me next to him on the wooden bench. "I'm sorry. No, it's not really Seamus, it's just…it's my parents."

His parents were the last thing I expected to hear. At the surprise on my face, he continues.

"A phone number ruined my family. My dad always wanted us to be…perfect. And no matter what my mom and I did, it never seemed good enough. But we tried. Then after one of my dad's military trips, my mom found a phone number in his pants pocket while she was doing the laundry."

"Oh, no." I can see where this is leading.

"Yeah. He was having an affair. He wasn't traveling at all, but rather being with this other woman. And it wasn't the first time."

"Oh, Finn, I'm so sorry."

"Well, my mom had enough and threatened to leave if he didn't break it off. He agreed, but not because of us—he just couldn't stand to be embarrassed among his friends. That's when we left for Ireland."

The abruptness of Finn's departure from school makes sense now. No wonder he's on edge about this number thing.

"I'll get rid of Seamus's number, Finn. Honestly, it doesn't mean anything."

"No," he says quickly. "I don't want you to. It's me that has to move on. I don't want to be like them. They haven't been the same since. Sure, they're still married but it's just an illusion. Like playing a part in a play."

I think about my parents and how devastated I would be if our family was torn apart by something like this. I lay my head on his shoulder and he wraps his arms around me. I promise myself that we will never be like them.

~

Come ten o'clock Saturday morning, Zoey is still snoring. Our girl's night was one for the books and we didn't fall asleep until around three. I sneak into the bathroom to call my sisters, but then I remember it's only about five in Maryland, and neither of them will be up yet. I call my mom instead. She's always up for the morning feedings by now.

She answers on the third ring, her voice bright. "Teagan! How are you, hon?"

A rooster crows in the background.

"Hi, Mom. Sounds like Frank hasn't changed."

"Nope. Craziest rooster I've ever known. Ashling set up an outdoor night light to work on her artwork and he crowed for a good ten minutes. And it was after nine."

I laugh, the picture clear in my head. Ashling setting up her easel, paint spread about. Frank shuffling back and forth, pride ruffling his feathers.

"We came up with a research idea this week."

"Is that so? What did you decide on?"

"Equine-assisted activities."

She squeals. "Really? That's wonderful."

"Yeah, I was wondering if you could send me the information from the presenter you and dad met during the conference."

"Sure. This is great, Teagan. I can't think of a better topic for you. And you're working well with your partner?"

I settle onto the floor and lean back against the wall. "You remember Finn, from high school chemistry?" I ask, knowing she will know exactly who I'm talking about. "Well, he's my partner."

The ensuing silence tells me she's letting this sink in. Kayleigh wasn't the only one who knew how hard it was to lose Finn. "Oh boy, you better start at the beginning."

After I fill her in on everything, I think about what Finn told me about his parents. It feels like a breach of trust to tell my mom about it, but Finn's story makes me wonder about *my* parents' relationship.

"Mom, you've always known you and dad were meant to be together, right? Like you guys have always been happy?"

"Sounds like you've been thinking a lot about love." she says, a smile in her voice. "Well, those are two very different questions, Teagan. Always being happy and knowing we're meant to be together aren't the same thing. Your father and I have had times when things were really hard, and happiness isn't always what you strive for. There are things more important than always being happy."

A heaviness takes up residence in my chest. "So, you're not happy?"

"Of course, we are happy, but happiness isn't everything. We've had times when we struggled."

"Like when?"

"Right after college, before we were married, we actually separated for a time. We were both working in different states and things got really hard. The long distance was hurting us."

All my life, I had pictured them being in touch every day, talking about their plans for their future farm, but they were not even together. "So, since then?"

"We've had our highs and lows, like any relationship. We have some big issues and little ones. Whether or not to open the animal rescue was one of them. And little things, like I can't stand the old lounger your dad put in the living room. You know, the one from his college dorm?"

I laugh, thinking about the ugly yellow and orange plaid chair that Dad loves so much.

"A relationship, any relationship, takes work, sweetie. It takes sacrifice and understanding. When you know in your heart you are meant to be together, you promise to always work on things. You promise in good times and in bad to love each other, and because of that, you grow stronger and stronger each day."

Maybe thinking their relationship was perfect actually took away from the beauty of it. Could their marriage be as strong as it is because it's not perfect?

I think about the horses I've helped my parents train over the years. It always seemed the ones that required the most work made me feel the best at the end. Like all of the hard work was really worth something. It meant so much more than just those daily drills or lessons, and it made something lasting.

I'm not sure what will happen with Finn, but I do know that I want something lasting too.

Chapter Nine

Sunday afternoon is the summer festival at the local Catholic parish, St. Patrick Church. Nora is selling her homemade rhubarb and ginger jam, as well as her blackberry and apple jam, both of which are absolutely delicious. A nervous energy vibrates in the air as everyone packs for the event.

"The office in the barn was a mess this mornin'." Nora fills the last of the jars.

"What do you mean?" I ask.

"Went in there lookin' for my tags, and the drawers of the desk were open, papers sticking out. Folders out of order in the file cabinet and the fancy laptop Seamus insisted we needed—gone. Nowhere to be seen. Disappeared in the wind."

Finn and I exchange a look. This isn't the first time Nora and Malachy have mentioned things being amiss around the farm. Papers gone missing or things moved about. A brand-new saddle disappeared last week and hasn't been found.

"Have you contacted the police?" Finn asks.

"Ah, no. No need to get the garda involved yet. Malachy insists there must be a reason. I worry Malachy is losin' his mind a bit and forgets what he's doin'. Thinks he may even have given the laptop to Seamus to set up that virus program."

"An antivirus protection program?" Finn asks.

"That's it. Nuisance it is. Don't trust havin' our information there for everyone to see."

"I didn't know Seamus was at the farm. Sorry to have missed him." *Why wouldn't he have visited with us?*

"Aye," Nora explains, "stopped by for a couple hours to help Malachy with the computer a few days ago. You two were in Dublin. Said he was sorry to miss you."

We'd made a quick trip to the Emerald Isle library for our research. How unfortunate that the one time we were away from the farm, Seamus came to visit.

Nora pats her apron. "Finn, would you be a dear and fetch the jar tags from the cottage closet? They must be there."

"Of course." Hesitation laces his voice, and he sends me a concerned look.

Something's not right.

I let out a sigh when he leaves through the back door.

"Young love." She smiles, loading the sink with used pots and utensils. "I remember those days. Malachy was quite the romantic back then."

"Really?"

"Aye." Her eyes sparkle. "He would come home, wildflowers spillin' out of those clumsy hands—"

"Nora!" Malachy calls. "Time to leave."

"Oh, dear." Nora's eyes widen at the mess in front of her.

"Why don't you two go down awhile. I'll clean this up and help Finn find the tags. We'll meet you there."

"You sure?"

"Yes, it's no problem."

"Thank you, my dear." Nora gives me a big hug, the scent of rose water lingering in the air.

I help load the rest of the jars into the wagon and watch the couple walk down the narrow lane. The parish is only a half mile away, so it shouldn't take us long to catch up. I hurry to clean up the kitchen.

"Finn? Any luck finding the tags?" I call through the cottage door about ten minutes later. When there's no response, I let myself in and find Finn sitting on the floor outside the closet, a piece of paper in his hands.

"Finn?"

He startles. "Oh, Teagan. It's you."

"Yeah. What are you doing? I thought you were looking for the tags for the jars."

He blushes. "I was, but when I pulled this box off the top shelf, I noticed something sticking out from a crack in the back wall. When I pulled on it, this envelope slid through."

He hands me a yellowed envelope. *The Kavanaghs* is written in black script across the center. The long strokes and curves resemble the fountain pens Ashling uses in her word art.

"It's a letter from Enrique Diaz to Eamon, Malachy's father."

I look from the letter to Finn in disbelief. His expression tells all.

"Can I see it?"

He passes the letter to me as I sit down beside him.

Dear Eamon,

    Words cannot express our gratitude to you and Roisin for your kindness over the past two years. Without you, Darlisa, Luciana, and I would be lost today instead of being given the opportunity to reunite with our family. While words are insufficient, there is something we want you to have. It has been in our family for more generations than I can count. It is not only a thank you, but a wish for future happiness. It is a priceless treasure—the Diaz Emerald. Save it for your rainy day. Let it bring you the sunshine you deserve.

Speaking of sunshine, our dearest Luciana, the sunshine of our life, wants you and Roisin to keep her locket to remember us always.

With sincerest gratitude,
Enrique Diaz

"The tale is true," I murmur.

"And buried in one of the fields on this farm." Finn's gaze is fixed, but I don't think he's seeing anything. Absently, he taps a corner of the envelope on the floor, and a little gold necklace slides out.

"A locket..." Speaking more to myself than to Finn, who's still lost in space, I gently open the dainty gold clasp, the hinge creaking slightly as it extends. Three happy faces smile at me from a faded photograph.

Finn shakes his head. Apparently he wasn't as far away as he'd seemed. "The Kavanaghs have never seen this."

"You think all of this has anything to do with what's happening on the farm?"

Finn shrugs. "I don't know, but I think we're going to find out soon."

The dread in his voice does nothing to soothe the frayed nerves that Nora's announcement left.

"Let's find the Kavanaghs."

~

The festival is bustling when we arrive. People stroll around a collection of fifty or so tables, selling everything from soda bread to Guinness to woolen scarves. Laughter rings through the air as we squeeze through the crowd in search of the Kavanaghs.

"Watch out!" A guy barks when I bump into him.

"I'm sorry. I didn't—"

"Teagan? Fancy seein' you here."

Recognition finally comes. Seamus's friend from the pub. "Oh, Ryan. Hi." I squirm as he stares at me a moment too long.

"Have you seen anythin'?" Fiona asks, eyeing the crowd.

"Hey, Fiona." Finn's greeting causes her to start.

"Finn. Teagan. Fancy seein' you two here."

Fiona looks more surprised than I would expect, considering we're living in Cloverdale. It's more surprising to see her here.

"Ah, yeah. It's just a short walk from Brigid's Crossing," I tell her. "I didn't realize you would be here today."

"Ah, right," Fiona waves her hand. "Family in these parts. Just a stone's throw away. Always come for the festival."

Ryan's eyes narrow at the envelope clasped in my hand. "Mailin' a letter home?"

"Oh, no. I mean, yes. To my sisters. Forgot to put it in the post." I sound like a child caught stealing a piece of candy.

"I could post it for ya." Ryan reaches for the envelope.

"No!" I shove it into my bag. "I've decided to add a note about the festival before I mail it. I'll do it on my way back."

Ryan's eyes run over me once again, sending a cold shiver down my spine.

"Fi, we should be goin'." Ryan wraps an arm around her waist and pulls her away. "Don't want to miss the pie-eatin' contest."

"Ye don't want to miss it." Fiona gives him a playful push. "I would be grand without it."

"Have fun!" I call in what could only be considered a screech.

Fiona sends me a concerned look, but before she can say anything, Finn grabs my hand. "Good seein' ya two." He pulls me in the opposite direction.

When we disappear in the crowd, Finn leans down and whispers in my ear. "What's going on? You're acting weird."

"I wonder why Fiona didn't mention she has family here."

Finn shrugs. "Maybe she never thought about it. I get the feeling everyone knows everyone and has family everywhere around here."

"True." He's right, but it doesn't settle my nerves. "Ryan just always makes me feel on edge. Why does Fiona hang out with him? They seem so different."

"Maybe they're related somehow."

"I doubt it, the way I saw them together at the pub."

"Who knows? Could be a third cousin or something. I have never known people had so many cousins before coming to Ireland."

The memory of our cab driver stopping in the middle of the road to talk with a friend and then a passerby comes to mind. Everyone seems so connected. While common here in Ireland, I rarely remember seeing people at home just stop to talk without a care to the time or schedule. Everything there moves at a quicker pace. There never seems to be time to just 'gab' with a neighbor or passerby.

"I kinda wish it was a little more like that at home," I admit to Finn.

"Yeah. I know what you mean. The roads are like racetracks and no one stops just to talk." After a pause he looks serious again. "So, what's going on?"

Embarrassment creeps in. "I don't know what came over me. I guess it feels wrong that we have the letter and the necklace. A part of me wishes we didn't know anything about the emerald. That you never found the envelope and we aren't involved in whatever's happening at the farm."

Finn squeezes my hand. "But we did find it, Teagan."

"Yeah." The weight of the situation hits me hard. "I guess we should look for Malachy and Nora."

Finn watches me carefully before a smile teases his lips. "Yeah, we should. But why don't we get one of those brown-bread ice creams first?"

"Now, that's a plan." And for a brief moment, I forget the tangled web we've gotten ourselves into.

~

Not long after, we find the Kavanaghs cleaning up Nora's table.

"There ye are." Nora waves to us.

The tags. We completely forgot about them in our discovery of the letter.

"Sorry, Nora, the tags weren't in the closet," Finn says, as if thinking the same thing. "But we did find something else."

Malachy raises a brow.

"What's goin' on?" Nora asks, concern creasing her forehead. "Did somethin' happen to ye?"

"Oh, no. We're fine. It's just that Finn found something." I pull out the envelope.

"I found it coming out of the wall at the top of the closet in the cottage. It was already opened," Finn explains.

I let out a breath as Malachy takes the envelope and adjusts his readers. "Never seen this before."

"Well, go on with ya." Nora waves her hand. "Open it."

As if sensing the significance, Malachy takes his time removing the letter. After slowly unfolding it, he smooths the creases. Nora's hands go to her hips and she purses her lips. Somehow I know it's taking every ounce of her self-constraint to not snatch the envelope from his hands.

"Oh, Nora."

Her eyes widen. "What?"

He hands her the letter, and she gasps. "Ah, the Lord!" She crosses herself. "It can't be."

"'Tis."

And with one more look they throw the rest of their supplies into the wagon, and we hurry back to the farm, the fastest pace I've experienced in Ireland yet. Malachy and

Nora rush through the cottage doors, leaving the wagon abandoned in the driveway.

We hear Nora's cry a moment later. "In the name of the Father, Son, and Holy Ghost …"

Hurrying inside, we stop dead at the sight before us. The contents of the closet are strewn about the floor, haphazardly discarded. Large, gaping holes are cut into the closet walls, exposing the drywall and studs.

A low throb takes root in my head as Finn murmurs, "I don't think we're the only ones looking for the emerald."

~

The next evening, we make a quick trip to Dublin in hopes of speaking with Seamus. We're trying to find any new clues regarding the emerald. It's good to see Finn acting warmly toward Seamus. His positive behavior reaffirms that we've grow even in these short few weeks.

"Tayto sandwich?" Seamus asks.

"What?"

"A tayto sandwich? Taytos in slices of buttered bread. A tayto sandwich."

"Okay, sure. Why not?" I laugh. When in Ireland…

"I'll have one too," Finn says as he joins us.

"Right." Seamus raises an eyebrow. "Be back in a bit."

As he disappears into the kitchen, I study Finn. This is the first time he's ever said two words to Seamus. Well, four words actually.

"You think Seamus can really help us with the emerald?" He stares at the kitchen doors.

"I don't know, but it can't hurt to ask. He's close to Malachy and Nora and they trust him with their whole hearts."

"Maybe that's the problem."

"What do you mean?"

"The Kavanaghs are great, but I think they're too trusting. They won't even consider the idea that someone could be taking advantage of them."

"And you think Seamus is the one taking advantage of them?"

He considers this before answering. "I don't know. Probably not."

"It has to be someone else." I make my voice firm. "I trust Seamus."

Finn slowly spins the coaster on the table. "Okay. You still think we should talk to him then?"

"Definitely."

Before we can discuss it anymore, Seamus returns with our sandwiches. I motion him close.

"Do you think we can talk to you about the—about something? Privately?"

Seamus's gaze bounces between the two of us. "Right. I have a break in a few. We could step outside."

"That would be great. Thanks."

He narrows his eyes before heading back to the bar to pour another round of pints for a table of rugby players. By the time we finish our sandwiches, which are surprisingly delicious, Seamus is pointing to the door. We follow him out into the cool night.

He looks at me expectantly.

"We have some questions about the emerald and are hoping you can help us."

Confusion crosses his face. "The Kildare emerald? From the tale?"

"Yeah, except it's not just a tale." I lower my voice. "We found a letter from Enrique Diaz to Eamon which proves he gave it to Malachy's parents."

Seamus just stares at me. "Ye serious?" He says a little too loudly, looking back and forth between us.

I grab his arm and urge him into the alley on the side of the pub.

"We think someone is trying to steal the emerald. Someone's been going through things at the farm. And, to make it worse, it feels like someone is watching us."

Seamus is speechless.

Finn pulls me closer, his warmth creating a safe haven. "Is there anything about the emerald you didn't tell Teagan already?"

"Got me. Been hearin' tales of that emerald since I was a lad. Never heard of a letter before."

"Yeah, Malachy and Nora were surprised too."

He frowns at the disappointment evident on our faces. "I do remember there was a lad Malachy always spoke of. Sean? Talked of their treasure huntin' days. He may know somethin'."

"Does Malachy stay in touch with him?" I'm hopeful that another connection may lead to new clues.

Seamus merely shrugs.

At that moment, something catches my eye. A shadow lurking by the corner of the building. I nudge Finn and Seamus, nodding my head at the form.

"I think it's time we go." Finn eyes both ends of the alley.

We follow Seamus toward the front of the pub.

"Is this a good idea?" I murmur to Finn. He takes my hand and pulls me behind him.

The screech of a woman's voice causes me to bump into Finn.

Seamus laughs. "Fiona? What're ya doin' out here?"

"Getting a bit of fresh air. What are ye doing back there? Nearly scared the life right out of me."

"Showin' 'em Mahoney's. Best shrimp in all of Ireland." He grins at us.

"Sounds great. We'll have to check 'em out, right, Teagan?"

"Y- yeah. That would be great." My voice is unsteady, and Fiona watches me, concern clouding her eyes.

"I think we're going to call it a night." Finn leads us back to the truck.

As we drive away, my skin crawls and tingles. Someone *is* watching us.

~

Sunday morning, a heavy silence blankets the farmhouse. Nora serves boxty while murmuring a rhyme under her breath.

"Boxty on the griddle,
Boxty on the pan.
If ya can't make boxty,
Ya'll never get a man."

"What's boxty?" I ask Finn under my breath.

"A traditional Irish potato pancake. They make it from leftover mashed potatoes and grated raw potatoes. It was a favorite of mine when my dad was stationed in Ireland."

I take a bite, letting the savory filling warm me. "It's good."

"Nora makes the best boxty 'round." Malachy places a kiss on Nora's cheek before settling into a chair at the kitchen table.

"Any sign of Tommy?" she asks. "Food will be gettin' cold."

"Not a trace."

"Never skips breakfast. And what about Mass? Always walks with us."

Malachy sighs. "He's a grown man, Nora. Let him be."

"He may be a man, but I've never known a man who didn't need a woman making sure he's fit as a fiddle."

I smile at the obvious care and affection they hold for Tommy. While we've been here for over a month now, I haven't really had much time to get to know their farm hand.

Nora and Malachy begin bickering about Father Nolan's recent homily, and I try to hold back a laugh.

Finn leans in and whispers close to my ear. "These two can find anything to argue about."

"It's endearing."

"That's one way to describe it."

"So what is Tommy like? I really don't know anything about him."

"Me neither. We may be staying in the cottage together, but he keeps to himself. We've barely said more than a few words to each other in passing."

"I wonder how he, Ryan, and Fiona became friends. They all seem so different. Nora mentioned the other day that Fiona and her boyfriend stopped by to pick Tommy up."

"Is Ryan her boyfriend?"

"I'm guessing he is."

"They do make an odd group." Finn leans close again. "I stayed up researching the Diaz's last night. The only surviving family member is Antonella Leon, the granddaughter of Luciana."

"Antonella. Should we contact her?"

"Already did. Sent her an email last night, so we'll see what happens."

"You think she'll know anything?"

"Don't know. But either way, hopefully we can return the necklace to the family at least."

"I'm still surprised Eamon wouldn't have put the necklace somewhere safe instead of leaving it in that envelope."

"I know. Maybe it was too hard. Seems like the families were really close."

"And the memory may have been too hard to face every day." I think of how the memory of Finn at school made my heart ache every day. I thought I'd never see him again.

"Malachy has gone to fetch Tommy, so we can be off." Nora heads out the front door, her yellow rain slicker tied snuggly around her waist, black umbrella in hand. She waves at us with the umbrella and we follow her like little ducklings following their mother. Finn takes my hand, not letting it go until we reach the church.

We are halfway through the second reading when Malachy and Tommy slide into the pew next to us. Father Nolan walks out in front of the altar to give his homily. Over the past few weeks, I've grown very fond of him and his way of preaching. His tall stature could come across as intimidating, but his youthful, dark curly hair and fast smile make him come across more as a friend than anything else. He's easy to talk to and captures our full attention when he speaks.

"The parable of the prodigal son is one of the most well-known and discussed of all time." He smiles at the congregation. "We often look at it from the son's point of view, but today let's look at it from the father's."

Tommy fidgets next to me, twisting his hands around and around.

"The younger son squanders his life's inheritance on the unholy. He's reckless, selfish, and on the path to becomin' a lost soul. We've all been there or know someone who has. When he realizes his sins and where he finds himself, he yearns to eat like the pigs on his father's land. You could say he hit rock bottom."

Tommy's knee jumps, then begins to bounce up and down, shaking our pew in the process.

"People will sometimes say the one good thing about rock bottom is that there's only one way to go—up. But that's not entirely true because you can dig below that rock. You can keep diggin' yourself into a deeper and deeper hole."

Tommy makes a whimpering sound.

"In the end, our boy makes a choice, and thankfully for him and his father, it's the right choice. He runs home askin' for forgiveness and a second chance, which his father readily grants him, and also welcomes him home in celebration. That's how Our Father wants to welcome each and every one of us. When we find ourselves at rock bottom, we have a choice to make. Are we going to keep diggin' ourselves into a deeper hole? Keep movin' farther and farther into the darkness? Or do we acknowledge our sins and ask our Father for forgiveness? If we choose the latter, we will get to live in the light of our Lord."

Tommy sways to the side, bumping into me.

"Tommy, are you okay?" I whisper.

Sweat dampens his brow, and his eyes appear red and glassy. I lean over Finn to get Nora's attention, but in doing so, release the support for Tommy. He collapses to the ground amid gasps and cries, blood dripping from his nose.

Chapter Ten

"Hello?" I answer an unknown number later that afternoon.

"Teagan, it's Nora."

"Oh, Nora. So glad it's you. Is Tommy okay?"

"He will be. Doc thinks he's sufferin' from exhaustion and anxiety. He believes it caused his collapse. Bloody nose from the fall. Poor lad." She sounds exhausted.

"Can I do anything to help?"

"Would ye mind doin' Shannon's session on ye're own tonight?"

"Of course, we can do it. Don't worry about us. We have it under control."

"Thank you, dear."

"Tell Tommy we hope he's better soon."

"Will do."

After getting off the phone with Nora, I knock on the cottage door. Finn answers, looking as miserable as I'm feeling.

"Nora called. Tommy's going to be okay. The doctor's said it's exhaustion and stress."

"Glad he'll be okay."

We exchange a strained look. After watching Tommy being taken away in the ambulance, we couldn't help but think drugs might be involved. He often acts like he's on edge, checking his surroundings—almost like a paranoia or something. A nagging guilt lingers. I was so quick to judge Tommy.

"Nora asked if we could do Shannon's session alone today."

He runs a hand through his messy hair. "Sure. Let me grab my boots and we can get the ring ready."

I wait for him on the front porch as a gentle rain begins tapping on the roof.

Finn steps up on the porch and gives me a long look. Something's up.

"What is it?"

"Earlier today, when you and Nora were helping with Tommy at the ambulance, Malachy mentioned Seamus called him about the emerald. They talked about stories from Malachy's childhood days, and Seamus asked about Sean."

I hold my breath. Will this be the clue we need?

"Malachy gave me Sean's address. Said he never answers the phone, so our best bet would be to visit him. Said he would do it himself, but with Tommy and everything, now he doesn't think he can."

"We should go," I say, without a second thought.

Finn grins. "I was hoping you'd say that."

And on that note, we head over to the stable.

~

"Shannon, ye're doin' such a great job!" Brianna calls from the side of the ring. Pride for her daughter rings in her voice.

The smile on Shannon's face grows at her mother's words. She's gripping the reins and leaning forward slightly in the saddle. Her legs are secured with bands on either side, and her boots safely point heel down in the stirrups. The boots were a present from her grandmother after seeing how the riding lessons brought Shannon such joy. Dirt smears now streak the shiny black leather, a sure sign of a good ride.

"You are amazing," Finn tells Shannon. The pride in his voice almost matches her mother's.

Finn is Shannon's side walker during the sessions. His job is to walk alongside the horse and assist the child in maintaining balance and proper form. While I'm instructing Shannon and leading Sam, Finn's job is to keep the rider safe on the horse. He rests his arm again her leg, helping to increase emphasis on using her muscles and also to hold her in place. He's the physical and emotional support for her and Shannon seems about as taken with Finn as she is Sam. The friendship is growing into something so very special, and it warms my heart watching them together.

We circle the ring one more time while Finn and I encourage our little charge to squeeze her legs and rise slowly in the saddle by pushing into her stirrups. Sam is a great match for Shannon. He's attuned to her movements and doesn't overreact when she applies too much pressure or gives him confusing signals. He's following my lead as I hold the lead rope. When our program officially begins, I'd love to add a horse leader to our team to maintain control of the lead rope and focus on the horse. That will free me, as the riding instructor, to work freely with the health or mental health professional during the session and have a larger view of their movement and progress.

All in time. Patience is something I'm still working on.

After the session is over, Finn walks Shannon back to Brianna while I lead Sam into the pasture, where he immediately joins Gandalf and begins grazing. I return to the beautiful sound of laughter as Shannon wraps her arms around Finn. He gently brushes the hair out of her face and gives her a massive bear hug back.

"I can't thank ye enough." Tears well in Brianna's eyes. "Shannon has never been happier." She hands me the pot pie she' baked as payment. The Irish people have such a beautiful way of turning a business or professional relationship into a friendship. I see why Nora and Malachy say everyone around here is family. They are a family of choice.

"It's our pleasure," I tell her.

"I see improvement with her balance already. 'Tis amazin', truly."

"I know, it really is. See, the horse's gait mimics the human gait, so therapeutic horseback riding allows people with cerebral palsy, and others with abnormal gait patterns, a chance for their neuromuscular system to experience a typical gait pattern."

"I'm not learned in the sciences, so it all means little to me, but I see the effect it's having with my Shannon. And I have ye to thank for that. This program will be life changin' 'round here."

Finn and I exchange a look. Our program has never felt more real than right here, right now. On paper, the program looks promising and provides an opportunity for advanced scientific research in the area of equine-assisted activities, but real life is where its power can be seen the most.

After Brianna and Shannon leave the farm, Finn and I sit on the bench by the horse pasture.

"I never get tired of watching them in the field."

Finn stretches an arm around my shoulders and drops a kiss on my cheek. "What you were telling Brianna about the horse and human gait is incredible."

"Isn't it?" My voice shakes with excitement. I love being able to talk about the science of equine therapy with Finn. "When a horse walks, the multi-dimensional movement is cyclical and rhythmical. It's reciprocal, which promotes large motor functions and learning, eventually enhancing functional mobility."

Finn looks at me with admiration, causing heat to flush my face. I love knowing that he not only likes me, but respects me, as well.

"How did you learn all this?"

"Some from the research, but mostly my parents. I've been riding since I was five. My parents not only taught me how to ride, but also the science behind it all. If it wasn't for their teaching and the wonder it instilled in me, I don't think I would love science as much as I do." Seeing the interest in his eyes, I keep talking. "And I love being able to talk to you about all of this. I mean, not many people are willing to discuss science—we know that from high school."

He grins. "Ah, it was the best of times, it was the worst of times."

"That it was." I laugh at his reference to a British Lit essay.

He gently twirls a strand of my hair around his finger.

"Want to take a walk?" A spark of excitement lights his eyes.

"Sure." I push off the bench and stretch my arms up high.

A few minutes into our walk, a ping sounds from Finn's pocket, and he checks the notification.

"It's an email from Antonella Leon."

We sit on a broken-down stone fence as he opens the message.

Dear Finn and Teagan,

I cannot express my surprise at seeing your email! A very welcome surprise. I would love to talk and help in any way I can.

All my best,

Antonella

"I can't believe Luciana's granddaughter actually emailed." I shake my head, amazed at how things happened.

"Let's see if she can talk now." Finn sends a quick response.

Dear Antonella,

We would love to talk too. Would you be available to
FaceTime?

Sincerely,

Finn and Teagan

Her reply comes through in mere moments, and we're
calling her before we know it.

Three beeps sound before Antonella picks up. She's a
beautiful girl with tan skin, long, dark brown hair flowing
over her shoulders, and big brown eyes. I glance at my reflection and run a hand over my messy ponytail.

"Hola!" She says brightly. I'm thrown off for a minute,
and I guess it shows because she laughs. "Just kidding. I
speak English too."

We join in her laughter, breaking the tension.

"I'm Finn, and this is Teagan. We're so glad you have
time to talk." He throws me a questioning look at my silence.

"I'm not sure how much help I'll be." Antonella shrugs
one shoulder. "But this legend has enticed me since childhood, when my abuela told me stories."

"Anything you can tell us is better than nothing," I finally
say. "And it's great to meet you."

"Same." She smiles. I already like her. She has an open
and friendly way about her. "So are you two really on the
farm right now? Tell me everything you guys have found
out."

We spend the next few minutes filling her in on everything we've learned so far.

"We were wondering if you ever saw letters that Luciana
may have kept." I pull a wry face. "We know it's a long shot,
but you know we have to ask."

Recognition dawns in Antonella's eyes. "Yes! I do remember them. I kept a chest of abuela's old belonging with
my childhood things." Pain is obvious in her eyes.

"You two were very close?"

"Yes. She was really like a mother to me. My mother died when I was only two, and my father left soon after. Abuela took me in and raised me."

"She sounds like an amazing woman," Finn says.

Joy fills her eyes once more. "Yes, she was. I will look for the letters. And if I find anything, I'll let you guys know."

"Sounds great. Thanks, Antonella." Too bad she wasn't closer, so we could actually meet in person.

"I bet Malachy and Nora would love to speak with you too," Finn says.

And as soon as he says it, I have an idea. "You wouldn't be up for a trip to Ireland, would you?"

Wide-eyed surprise is quickly overcome with excitement. "I would love nothing more!"

And we begin making plans.

~

Two weeks later, Tommy is back on the farm, and the Kavanaghs have settled back into a routine. They could not believe we located Antonella and absolutely loved the idea of having her come and visit. She'll arrive in two days, and the anticipation has given the Kavanaghs a much-needed boost to their spirits. While Finn and I also look forward to meeting Antonella in person, we know that alone time with the Kavanaghs will be needed. So it seems perfect timing that this weekend we have another check-in at Emerald Isle.

Finn's brow furrows deeply as we add another section to the rough draft of our proposal.

"Okay, what's up?" I'm unable to concentrate with him sitting there staring off into space.

"I think Tommy's stealing from the Kavanaghs."

"What?" Disbelief is evident in my voice.

"I overheard him on the phone last night. It sounded like he was talking to a debt collector." He rubs his forehead in a circling motion, as if trying to push the tension away. "I don't think he knew I was here. He said he would have the money soon and asked for more time. Then he hurried out and slammed the door on the way."

I think of our recent interactions. "I wonder if he's in some kind of trouble. Maybe that's why he's so jumpy."

"Teagan, what if that's where the Kavanaghs' money is going? And the weird stuff happening at the farm. What if Tommy is stealing to pay off a debt?"

As much as I don't want to believe it, Finn makes a good point. "So…do we say something?"

Finn ruffles his hair in frustration. "I don't know. I don't know Tommy well, but I never thought he would steal from them. And I'm not sure the Kavanaghs would believe it either."

"Yeah, I know. They love him like a son."

"It will break their hearts if it turns out to be true."

"But if we don't tell them, they could lose the farm."

We look at each other, neither knowing the answer.

"Should we say something to Tommy first? Maybe you misunderstood the conversation?" I'm grasping at straws, hoping there's a logical answer that has nothing to do with the strange guy stealing from our hosts.

"Except…if it is true, then talking to Tommy is probably not the way to go."

I can't help but hear Ashling's voice. *Teagan, just do a little investigating on your own.* "Maybe we should…um, check his room and see if we can find anything."

Finn's expression is a mix of surprise and amusement.

"Then we will know if we should say something to the Kavanaghs." I blush but defend my idea. "If we say something and it's not true, the consequences would be awful."

"But if we know it is true, then" He doesn't have to finish—his look says it all.

We go as quietly as possible into Tommy's room, checking the windows to make sure he's not on his way back.

"He's not here. I'm not sure why we're tiptoeing around." A hint of humor colors Finn's voice.

"Well, I don't make a habit of this, so I'm not quite sure how to do it."

Tommy's things are scattered about the small room. His bed is unmade, and drawers hang open. I resist the urge to straighten it up and begin searching the dresser, while Finn takes the bed.

He throws the blanket back on top, then gets on the floor to search underneath. "Nothing here."

Tommy's drawers are full of mismatched socks and wrinkled clothes. "Seriously, how do guys live like this?"

"This may not be the best time to debate it."

"No debate necessary. I'm obviously right."

Finn laughs and continues searching through the small corner desk. I skip what appears to be an underwear drawer, shoving it closed before opening the top drawer. A few coins are scattered about with a pair of work gloves and some gum wrappers. A leather bracelet with a silver medallion is tucked in the corner.

"Finn, look at this."

Finn joins me. "Kinda dark."

"Yeah. I've seen this symbol before, but I can't remember where."

Sharp, twisted points form a crown with a snake arching out of the top, beady eyes staring from a triangular head. A chill runs the entire length of my spine.

"Teagan, look." Finn slides Tommy's jockey shorts to the side of the adjacent drawer.

I gasp at the sight of stacks of bills wrapped with rubber bands. "There must be over 5,000 euros in there."

"And more." The pain in Finn's voice is palpable.

I follow his gaze to the ledger for the farm. Finn turns the cover over and lying on top is a piece of paper with the Kavanaghs' banking account and routing information written on it. All in Tommy's handwriting.

"He's altered the books." Finn points to edited numbers in the farm supplies. "It goes back for months."

We jump at the creaking sound of the front door opening. Finn closes the drawer as quietly as possible, then nods toward the window. Tommy's boots clump down the short hallway. I can't move. Every nerve in my body is in overdrive and appears to have short-circuited.

Suddenly, a dog barks outside and the heavy footsteps stop.

"Ollie, what is it?" Tommy retraces his path to the front door. "Oh man, sheep are out again. I can't catch a break. Well, let's get 'em, boy." The front door closes, and we hurry out of the bedroom, the bracelet still in my hand.

Chapter Eleven

Antonella arrives the next day and the entire farm seems to brighten. The sun even chooses that moment to make an appearance. Our introductions are as warm as the weather, Antonella feeling like a member of the family from the start. Malachy and Nora take her on a tour of the farm, while Finn, Tommy, and I prepare the beef stew for dinner.

Finn and I tried to talk with the Kavanaghs this morning about Tommy, but they were so busy preparing for Antonella that they asked if we could speak tonight instead. While I want to tell them the truth as soon as possible, a part of me also wants to protect them. I know how much his betrayal will hurt. And maybe there's still a chance we have this all wrong.

While we're chopping vegetables, Finn finds a moment to question Tommy.

"So, how long have you been with the Kavanaghs?"

Tommy briefly glances at Finn, and then returns his gaze to the carrots he's slicing. "A little over a year now."

"Do you like working here?" I prompt him.

"Yeah." He's a man of few words.

"What brought you here?" Finn adds celery to the pot.

Silence—for so long that I wonder if Tommy's going to respond at all. "Work. I needed the job."

"Did you work anywhere before here?" I try to be as friendly as I can, hoping he will relax and open up a bit.

"I was in Limerick for a few months. Nothing there but trouble."

Finn and I exchange a look.

"What kind of trouble?" Finn asks.

"You name it, it's there." Tommy turns away from us as he empties the carrots into the stew and begins washing the cutting board and knife in the deep sink.

Not knowing whether to continue or not, I look to Finn. He's watching Tommy from the corner of his eye. "Understand that," Finn's voice sounds deeper than usual. "Had trouble myself, back in my hometown. Hard to get away from."

I throw Finn a questioning look and he gives a slight shake of his head.

"Yeah, I get that."

"My brother got into trouble with gambling. He was down so much he started stealing to pay it back."

Heat rises up my neck and prickles my face. I steal a glance at Tommy. Holding the knife under the water, he stares at it like it holds the answer. The hairs on my nape rise.

"Stew's all set. Let's set the table and get the drinks ready." I interrupt whatever Finn's about to say, and he doesn't seem happy about it, but I don't like where the conversation is leading. We work quietly until Antonella and the Kavanaghs return.

"This farm is incredible," Antonella gushes in her smooth, sultry accent.

"Tommy, come here and meet Antonella," Nora calls, her cheeks ruddy from the exercise.

Tommy stands frozen to the spot, eyes large. I find it hard not to laugh out loud at his reaction, which I bet is a common occurrence for Antonella. She walks over and sticks out a hand. "Hi, Tommy. Nice to meet you."

He finally smiles back. "Same to you." He continues holding her hand a bit too long, and Malachy clears his throat, causing them to finally release their hold.

Antonella sits in the empty seat on my right. "I brought the letters with me." Her whisper is loud enough for Finn to hear on the other side of me.

"Really? Did you read through them?" I completely forget about everything but the emerald.

"Yes. Nothing stands out to me, but maybe you will find something." She pulls a small bundle of papers out of her purse, and I slide it into my bag. The excitement in Finn's eyes matches my own, and I suddenly can't wait for dinner to end so we can read the letters.

"It's as if Luciana has returned. Ye're a spittin' image of her, my dear." Malachy's smile warms his craggy face.

Antonella's cheeks pink a bit, making her beauty even more radiant.

"Right ya are," Nora agrees. "Dear, we have somethin' we'd like ya to have." She reaches into her pocket and pulls out the gold locket.

"What is it?" Confusion marks Antonella's features.

"Your grandma's necklace," Malachy tells her. "It's yours. Luciana would've wanted ya to have it."

Finn squeezes my hand. No matter what happens with our research proposal, we've made a difference here.

"Abuela," Antonella murmurs, running a finger over the photo in the heart. She fumbles with the clasp and Tommy jumps up to help her.

"Let me get that." He opens his hand.

She places the necklace in his rough palm and lifts the long hair off her neck. Tommy carefully secures the necklace, letting it drape down in front. The locket shines on

Antonella, looking like it was always meant to be there. The gold reflects the candlelight. Nora must have spent hours cleaning and buffing it to look as beautiful as it does now.

"Thank you so much." Tears brim in Antonella's eyes.

Malachy and Nora smile, looking like they've just met their new granddaughter. Knowing them, that may be exactly what they're thinking.

With that out of the way, we enjoy the best beef stew I've ever tasted.

~

I call Kayleigh and Ashling on our drive to Dublin the next day. They were waiting to hear all about Antonella and an update on Tommy. Having my sisters involved, even if across the world, provides more support than I imagined. As we bump along the muddy road, I find myself at a loss as to where to begin."

"Well…" I sigh into the phone. "After dinner last night, Malachy insisted on playing the fiddle and sharing so many stories about the farm that I feel like I've lived there my whole life. Antonella laughed along with us, very much at home with the Kavanaghs. But with all the festivities, it was near midnight when we finally settled in to read the letters." I sigh, even as I attempt to keep my frustration to a minimum. "Nothing stands out to us any more than it did for Antonella. The disappointment has left us feeling a little deflated."

"Oh no, Teagan. I'm so sorry," Kayleigh says with a sigh.

"Well…" Ashling hesitates, then dives right in, as is typical of my little sister. "What about the conversation with the Kavanaghs about Tommy?"

"Our conversation with the Kavanaghs was delayed till this morning because of the celebration, and when we finally told them everything, the biggest surprise was on us.

Malachy said he gave Tommy the ledger and put him in charge of helping to balance it."

"But what about all the money?" Ashling sounds as alarmed as I'm feeling.

"When we told them about the money, they couldn't believe it. So we went to the cottage with them." I close my eyes at the memory. "Tommy was doing the morning feeding, so he wasn't there. We went into his room, Finn pulled open the drawer…and it was all gone."

"What?" Kayleigh and Ashling shriek together.

"The money wasn't there. Nothing. Nada."

Finn's knuckles turn white as his grip tightens on the steering wheel.

"I don't understand," Kayleigh mumbles.

"Neither do we. We know it was there, so he must've known we were looking around his stuff. Maybe he noticed his bracelet missing."

"Well, you have to find it. Don't give up!"

"Ashling, I wish we could, but you don't understand. The Kavanaghs are so disappointed in us. Their eyes said it all. Tommy is like family to them."

"Family is important," Kayleigh agrees. "But so is the truth."

"Right on!" Ashleigh affirms. I can practically see her fist pumping in the air. "Wish I was there to help you guys."

Me too.

"We're just about to Dublin now, so I better go."

There's silence, and the frustration of not being able to talk to them whenever I want is getting to me. "Miss you guys, and I promise to call soon."

By the time I end the call, the Emerald Isle sign is in front of us. Time to focus on our research. If only I could get the image of the Kavanaghs out of my mind. The hurt in their eyes is enough to make me wish we'd never gotten involved with the emerald in the first place.

Our luck doesn't improve when we get to Fiona's office. The door is locked and a note with our names is taped on the center.

Teagan and Finn,
    So sorry to have to cancel our meeting today. Something has come up. We'll catch up in a couple days.

Fiona

"That's odd," I say. "It doesn't seem fair for her to just cancel."

"She couldn't have told us before letting us drive here in that mess?"

The rain has been nonstop all day. While rainy days are common, today is more on the monsoon level than a mere rainstorm—a perfect match for our moods.

Our phones ping simultaneously with a new text message.

"Kyle and Zoey want to meet in the pub for lunch." Finn raises an eyebrow.

"Sounds good to me."

He types a response and slides his phone into his back pocket.

As we huddle under an umbrella on the way to O'Callaghan's, my thoughts return to Antonella and the Kavanaghs. Have they found any clues about the emerald since we left this morning?

Escaping the worst of the rain, we hurry into the pub, and I toss my bag on the chair next to Zoey.

"Oh, your bracelet." Zoey picks up the black band and studies the medallion.

"It's not mine. I, er…"

"I've seen this. That's the same as Ryan's tattoo." Zoey pulls it closer to get a better look.

Ryan. That's why the symbol was familiar. I'd seen it when I met him that first night in the pub, the tattoo exposed from his shirt sleeve.

"I just found it," I say, more defensively than necessary.

Zoey doesn't seem to notice though. "It's kinda creepy." She hands it back to me.

"Yeah, I agree." I slide it into my bag as I change the subject. "Where's Maria?"

"Gone," Kyle says. "She left the program. Said it wasn't for her and she was ready to go home."

I think of Zoey and Kyle's proposed research based on the role of soil microbes in the sustainability of the Irish sheep farms. "Has that messed up your research?"

"Nah." Kyle shakes his head. "It's actually going much smoother without her." He and Zoey exchange a meaningful look.

"I'm sure you're happy to have more time alone now too," I tease.

"Sure, right about that!"

It's really nice to catch up with them, but Finn is quieter than normal.

"You okay?" I ask when Kyle and Zoey take to the dance floor.

"I heard Zoey say it looks like Ryan's tattoo."

I nod and hand him the bracelet. "Yeah. I remember it now. I wonder what it means."

"It's odd. I don't remember seeing it in any Celtic symbols I've seen." He turns it around, looking at it from every angle, before I slide it back into my bag.

We're about halfway through dinner when Seamus walks in. Ryan follows with a couple of buckets in his hands, and both of them are laughing. The distinct smell of dead fish and something just as familiar flows through the pub.

"Got some crab for ya, Teagan!" Seamus calls, holding a wood basket up.

"And I got my Crabby Spice!" I call back, holding up one of my little travel packets.

He shakes his head, laughing. "I'll get ya in a bit."

Seamus joins us a few minutes later, the scent of fish lingering on him. "Aye, sorry. Comes with the territory." He slides four crab cakes on the table.

"Oh, these look amazing." I sprinkle on the Crabby Spice.

Seamus scratches his head. "Americans."

I'm about to defend myself when I notice the black leather bracelet wrapped around his wrist—identical to the one in my bag. My heart sinks as I see the clear recognition in Finn's eyes. A quick shake of his head tells me we need to wait till we leave to talk about this, making it the slowest dinner in recent memory.

Just as we finish paying the tab, my phone rings and I jump. An unknown American phone number flashes on the screen.

"Hello?" I answer, still feeling a bit shaken.

"Hi, this is Dr. Kimberly Campbell. Is this Teagan?

"Yes. Hi, Dr. Campbell. My parents have told me so much about you."

Finn gestures out the window. The rain has stopped and the sun is shining, proving once again that Irish weather is unpredictable.

"Isn't that sweet. Well, your parents are two of the best vets I know. And even better people. I was delighted when they called and told me about your research idea."

Zoey and Kyle wave goodbye as we make our way to the park bench, then spread our rain jackets on the seat.

"Thank you." I put the call on speaker. "My friend, Finn, is here too. We would love to speak with you about setting up an equine-assisted activities program. My parents say you have one of the best programs out there."

"I'd love to. I have to warn you though—once you begin down this road, you'll never go back. The healings that I've seen with my own eyes are enough to completely dedicate the rest of my life to this mission. Little miracles every day."

Something warm flows through me. Something I can't put a name to, just an assurance that this is it.

"I think I'm speaking for both Teagan and myself when I say, tell us everything," Finn says. The three of us laugh in a way that makes me believe we're about to be part of something that will forever change our lives.

"Okay, let's start at the beginning." Dr. Campbell's voice takes on a more professional tone. "Horses have been working with humans for centuries. Equine therapy goes all the way back to the ancient Greeks. There are documents from Orbasis of ancient Lydia that describe the therapeutic value of horseback riding in 600 B.C. In more recent times, equine therapy was introduced in Scandinavia in 1946 during an outbreak of poliomyelitis. Therapeutic riding was officially established in the US and Canada in 1960 with the formation of the Community Association of Riding, or CARD. It was developed as a means of motivation for education and therapeutic benefits of the body and mind. Today we have a few top organizations that are leading the way into what I can only describe as a promising future."

"I never would've thought, before our research, that equine therapy started so long ago," Finn says.

"Can you explain the different types of equine activities you have in your program?" I start a bullet list in my notebook.

"Of course. Equine-assisted activities are activities provided by non-licensed professionals that utilize the inherent therapeutic benefits of being around horses to enhance non-clinical activities. You guys can eventually broaden your program to include equine-assisted therapy, equine-assisted counseling, or equine-facilitated psychotherapy, with a licensed health or mental health care professional. These are the programs I facilitate, and they can accommodate treatments such as hippotherapy and therapeutic horseback riding."

"My parents told me how amazing it is to watch patients on the horses and about the success they've had."

"Oh, yes. It is quite unlike anything I've ever seen. And Teagan, with your knowledge and background with horses, you would be a great candidate as a therapeutic riding instructor."

"I would love that."

"For you two and your research project, I would start with just equine-assisted activities, because it is something you could implement seamlessly in the Emerald Isle program next year, while you find professionals to partner with. This is what your mom has been doing, Teagan. And if you have instincts like hers, this program next year will be life-changing."

Next year. This is really happening. If we do win, we will be able to develop this program next year. My resolve is strengthening by the minute.

After speaking with Dr. Campbell for another half hour and promising her we will keep her posted on our research, Finn and I move to the Emerald Isle library and settle in to finish writing our proposal. We spend the next few hours typing and re-typing our ideas until we feel like we can't write another word.

When I finally climb into my bed in the dorm room, it's past midnight. Something changed in me when we spoke with Dr. Campbell. Even though we are deep into our research, hearing her confirm my beliefs about the program puts it in a new light. I know that whatever happens with our proposal, whether we are chosen or not, I want to create this program. And I know Brigid's Crossing is where it should be.

I pull out the journal Kayleigh gave me all those weeks ago, and flip through mostly empty pages. I take it as a sign…up until now there has been emptiness on these pages, a blank slate, but I am at a new beginning. Uncapping the pen, I press it to the paper.

Today, I begin to fill these pages with a new dream. A dream that I know will forever change my life.

I keep writing, lulled by the scritch-scratch of my scribbling, until my head hits the pillow hours later.

~

Finn and I arrive at the Mahoney's cottage around noon the next day, as arranged. The drive was a beautiful one, but overshadowed by the discovery of Seamus's bracelet last night. We debated whether it means anything or maybe the bracelets are just a popular item in the area. For all we know, they may sell them at all the local shops. As reassuring as the thought is, it doesn't explain the tattoo. There must be a meaning behind it, but after the fiasco with Tommy and the Kavanaghs, the last thing we want is to jump to conclusions again.

Rolling hills peppered with sheep lead to the little white cottage over the hill. As we roll down the drive, I imagine the picturesque scene easily hanging in an art gallery—though, on second thought, that type of atmosphere might be a little cold. Over the mantle of a fireplace perhaps, where it would make any room cozier with its warm, homecoming ambiance.

My thoughts are interrupted by the sight of a man leading a pony carrying a small boy on its back. The man waves us over and we walk toward the endearing pair. The boy looks to be about seven or eight. He has a thin frame with stiff movements. Heavy black glasses frame his eyes, and his mouth forms a large grin as he pats the pony's haunches. The animal looks back at him, pleasure evident in its big brown eyes.

The man stretches out a strong hand. "Sean Mahoney."

"I'm Finn and this is Teagan. Thanks for agreeing to meet with us."

"No bother. And this is our son's lad, James." Love glistens in his eyes, adding a soft edge to his rugged appearance. "Loves his time with ol' Hugo here." He nods to the pony.

"Is he a Kerry bog pony?" I ask, having read about them before the trip. While I've been around horses my whole life, I've never seen one of these. The Kerry bog pony evolved in the Irish heathland, where they lived feral lives in the peat bogs. Over the centuries, they started being used as draft horses, saving the backs of many hardworking farmers. Today it is recognized as the Heritage Pony breed of Ireland.

"Aye, you know your horses! Hugo, here, is the best one out there."

I run my hand over the animal's palomino coat and long blond mane. He looks to be between ten and eleven hands high, with a broad chest, muscular shoulders, and strong, compact body. His legs are short and defined with light-colored, freshly trimmed hooves. Hugo is well cared for, and this raises the Mahoney family even higher in my esteem.

"He's beautiful and so well-mannered." I watch James playing with his mane.

"That he is. Intelligent and sensible too. The whole package right here."

The pride in his voice is unmistakable.

"I can see that." It's true. There's no doubt this horse is very special, especially for James. They have a deep connection.

"Do ya have a horse?"

"Yes. Well, many actually. My family has a horse farm and animal rescue back in the U.S. My parents are both veterinarians and started Claddagh Farm and Animal Rescue in our small hometown in Maryland. While we have all kinds of rescues, horses hold a special place in my heart."

"Aye. Right you are. No creature like the horse."

I can tell Sean Mahoney is a man with a good heart, and now I can see why he and Malachy are such great friends.

"Do they ride together often?" Finn points to James, who's now lying forward, arms wrapped around Hugo's thick neck.

"All the time. See," he comes a little closer and lowers his voice, "James is what you'd call different. The fancy doctors call it autism. He keeps his distance from people but opens up with ol' Hugo here."

Finn and I exchange knowing looks. "Have you ever heard of equine therapy?" Finn asks.

And just like that we have another participant in our program. A lingering feeling of dread curls around my chest. If something happens to the farm, this program will disappear as quickly as the money from Tommy's drawer.

Chapter Twelve

As the sun begins its descent, the scent of roasted chicken drifts through the cottage, and my stomach responds with a grumble. I hadn't noticed how hungry I am until the aroma of the delicious roast Caitlin prepared wafts around me. When we're all seated at the table, Sean leads us in grace. We bow our heads, and a sense of peace settles over me. Why don't I regularly say grace before meals? Sure, on our Sunday dinners at home we say grace, but what about all the other meals? The absence now seems empty, and I promise myself to remember to pray before all my meals in the future. As I bite into the savory chicken for the first time, I send up another prayer of gratitude for this food and the people around the table.

"So, ye wanted to speak with us?" Sean asks.

I put my fork down. Continuing the search for the emerald is more daunting now, but with the possibility of the Kavanaghs losing the farm there isn't another option. "Yes, we were talking with Malachy and heard about your treasure hunting days at Brigid's Crossing. We were wondering if you could share anything you remember from those days."

Sean lets out a bellowing laugh. "Ah, those were the days. A couple of lads searchin' for mythical treasure."

Finn and I exchange a look. "We actually found a letter from Enrique Diaz to Eamon about the emerald. Malachy says it's proof that the emerald does really exist and is buried somewhere on the farm."

Sean's mouth hangs open. "Ye're tellin' me it's true?"

Finn and I nod together.

"Well, I'll be. Malachy has a real treasure hidden on that farm."

"We hope so," I say. "The Kavanaghs could really use it right now."

Concern edges Sean's eyes. "I've heard of their troubles. Wish we could help 'em." He nods to Caitlin.

"Wish we could," Caitlin agrees. "Never met more solid people. Shame what's happenin' to 'em."

"The only way we figure they can save the farm is if we find the emerald," Finn says.

"If anyone can find that emerald, bet it's ye. Sorry to say, it was all fun and games back in the day. Wouldn't know where to start with a real hunt."

Disappointment settles over me. I really thought Sean might hold the clue we are so desperate to find.

"I think to know where he buried it, ya need to know the man. If ya know his heart, ya know where his treasures lie," Caitlin says.

"Aye, very true."

"Of course," I say. "We need to learn more about Malachy's father to understand where he may have buried it. That makes sense."

Finn nods. "We've been searching all over the grounds, but without knowing him, we'll probably never know where it's buried."

"Maybe it's not buried in the ground." James takes a big spoonful of his pudding.

"Oh, dear, let me wipe your mouth." Caitlin gently wipes away the pudding from the little boy's mouth and kisses the top of his head, love evident in every movement.

We say our goodbyes to the Mahoneys and promise to pass on their well-wishes to the Kavanaghs. In return, they promise to bring James by the farm for a riding session when the program is up and running.

"Hope ye find ye're treasure," Sean calls as we pull away. James hugs his granddad's leg with one arm and waves wildly with the other. Hugo watches the boy from the fence, ears perked in his direction.

And for the first time, I think I just might find my real treasure after all.

We return to Brigid's Crossing just before midnight, but instead of feeling tired, I'm wide awake.

"Everything okay?" Finn asks, as he locks the truck.

"Yeah. I'm just not ready for bed yet."

"Same." He looks around. "There's a fire pit by the cottage."

"Perfect."

The wood feels dry, and the wind has calmed enough that we may be able to start a fire, but we don't have matches.

"I did make Eagle Scout," Finn tells me with unabashed confidence. "I've got this."

Of course he did. If anyone was going to be an Eagle Scout, it would be Finn. And just like that, we had a fire. He slowly blows on the kindling, and the small flames wave, reminding me of the Bunsen burners from chemistry.

A memory flows through my mind like the smoke from the embers. Finn and I were at our bench, prepping for an ionic compound lab, when our hands brushed, sending sparks cascading over my skin.

"I think I'm starting to believe in love at first sight."

Finn adds the rest of the sticks before sitting beside me. "I hope you aren't talking about someone you met recently."

A laugh escapes my lips. "No. More like someone I met a long time ago, thought was gone forever, and then showed up again when I least expected him."

"Sounds familiar. Wonder if I know him."

This is what I missed most when Finn left. Our conversations were always so natural.

"What are you thinking?" His caramel eyes peer into mine as if searching for the answer.

"I was just thinking about chemistry."

His face is expectant, and he waits for me to continue.

"The fire just reminded me of a day that our hands brushed during lab. I know it sounds crazy, but it's like I knew we were… meant to be."

"The ionic compound lab."

"You remember."

He brushes the hair away from my eyes. "Like it was yesterday. So, you do believe in love at first sight now?" He leans over and kisses me for a long moment.

When my eyes open, I consider him and our relationship. My heart feels like it's expanding each time I look into his eyes. "Well, no. I still don't think you can fall in love just from seeing someone. But I believe God puts certain people in our lives for a reason. Sometimes that's for romantic love, sometimes friendship, sometimes for reasons we aren't aware of."

"Which do you believe God intends for us?"

The hope in his voice is almost too much and the walls around my heart crumble dangerously. I lean over and kiss him again. "Romantic, friendship, and more than we could ever imagine."

"I love you, Teagan. I always have."

"I love you too. My heart broke when you left school, but now it feels like it's healing."

"Teagan, I owe you an explanation. I never wanted to leave. My dad told us the night before, and I was furious with him. We didn't speak for a long time, and you know why." I see the pain in his eyes, and I wish there were some way to make it go away. "I wasn't in a place to understand my feelings or know how to handle them. I was wrong not to say goodbye or explain what was going on, but I didn't want to accept any of it. So, I figured if I cut off ties, I could get over you…but it only made it worse. I'm so sorry."

I wrap my arms around his waist, and he pulls me close. Laying my head against his chest, I listen to his heartbeat. "I understand, Finn."

He tucks a stray hair behind my ear. "I promise to never hurt you again."

He kisses me, and all thoughts of the past fade away.

~

I awake a couple hours later to the sound of screams outside my window.

"Malachy, the Fire Brigade!"

The Dublin Fire Brigade?

I jump out of bed and run to the window. Dark black plumes of smoke bellow into the sky.

The cottage.

A scream escapes my lips as I run down the steps and out the back door. The moment I'm outside I take in the scene. A team of fire fighters from the Cloverdale Volunteer Fire Department work to pull the water hoses toward the cottage, while several others gear up for a rescue. An ambulance waits, lights flashing, as a stretcher is wheeled into the back. The doors slam shut, and they take off down the drive, siren blaring. A couple EMTs stay behind, setting up a workstation.

Nora hurries to Antonella's side, wrapping her arms tightly around her. I run to them as fast as my legs will take me.

"Where's Finn?" I scream.

Nora and Antonella turn to me, tears sliding down their soot-covered faces. Nora pulls me into their embrace. "He made it out but is unconscious. They're taking him to Dublin." She crosses herself and begins praying the rosary.

"Tommy's still in there," Antonella whispers, fright straining her voice. Nora lets out a sob between prayers.

"Teagan, it was those men. The men in black." Antonella looks at me with stricken eyes. Her head falls to Nora's shoulder.

We follow the EMTs to the hospital. Malachy goes in with Tommy while we settle in the waiting room. When a nurse comes out, they tell us Finn has some smoke inhalation and is dehydrated but should make a full recovery. They allow me to go to his room, and the sight of him is almost too much.

Lying on the bed, IV hanging from his arm, he looks so fragile. The scent of smoke lingers in the air. His eyes are swollen, and he adjusts the uncomfortable-looking oxygen tube in his nose.

"Oh, Finn." I hug him the best I can without messing the tubes up. "It's so good to see you." Sitting on the bed next to him, I stroke his bandaged hand.

"Just mild burns," he reassures me. "Nothing big. Doctor said I should be able to go home tomorrow."

The farm is home now.

"I'm so glad."

"We made sure the fire was out, right, Teagan?" Finn's pained expression is enough to send my anger boiling.

"Finn. We did not cause this fire. It was out when we went to bed. Remember? We poured water on it and everything."

"Yeah, I know, but how else could it have started?"

Antonella's words come back to me. "That's what I'm going to find out." I kiss his forehead. "I'll be back soon. You just worry about getting some rest. I love you."

"Love you, too."

A nurse walks in the room. "Finn, ya ma is on the phone. Do ya feel up to talkin' to her?"

Finn nods and the nurse connects the call to his phone.

After closing the door quietly behind me, I stride to the waiting room with renewed determination. I spot Antonella right away. She's sitting in a corner, sipping a coffee, while Nora knits beside her.

"Finn?" Nora asks when I join them.

"He's doing okay Doctor is saying he should be released tomorrow. They want to hold him for observation and give him fluids."

"Thank the Lord!" She puts her knitting aside and promises to bring us back a "good meal" from the hospital. Unless hospital food is different in Ireland, I don't think she's going to have much luck with that. But her absence gives me a chance to talk with Antonella alone.

I sit down in Nora's seat. "Antonella, earlier you said something about two men. What did you mean by that?"

She closes her eyes for a moment before looking at me. "Yesterday afternoon, I was with Tommy on the cottage porch. We were playing cards when these two motor bikes came speeding into the driveway. The men were dressed all in black and looked like trouble. I've seen my fair share of thugs back in Colombia, and I got that feeling, you know?"

I nod, understanding exactly what she means. I remember the two men that walked into the pub that night. Same description. Seamus said they were Nathair men. Could Tommy somehow be mixed up with the gang?

"They gave me the creeps. After interrupting us, one of the men grabbed Tommy's arm and pulled him down the steps and to the side of the cottage. I shifted my chair so I could still see them. I couldn't hear anything, but they were threatening him. I'd bet my life on it. Pushed him to the ground and rode off on their motorbikes. Tommy was trembling when he came back over. Whatever they said to him shook him up. Then the fire just a few hours later…it's not a coincidence."

"No, it doesn't sound like it is."

~

The next morning, we wish Antonella safe travels on her flight home. It feels like a part of our family here is leaving. Her visit was way too short, but in that brief time, she became a part of us. It's odd that the notion of family has changed so much. Before coming to Ireland, I never thought I could find a community like we have at home, but now that I'm here, I feel like I belong in both places.

I call my mom to update her on everyone. She'd been beside herself with worry after she heard about the fire. I'm sure she's gotten about as much sleep as we have since it happened.

"Teagan, how are you doing, baby?"

"I'm okay, Mom. Malachy is on his way home with Finn and Tommy. The smoke inhalation was the worst of it, and he's steadily improving."

"Has Antonella already left?"

"Yeah, she was distraught leaving, but at least she knows everyone is going to be okay. I already miss her."

"I'm sure you do."

We sit in comfortable silence for a moment before she continues. "Are you still giving your presentation on Friday?"

That's only a couple days away and it's starting to hit me that we'll soon learn about the research position. Luckily I have a copy of our proposal on my laptop. Finn's was lost in the fire, with most of his other belongings.

"Yeah, we're ready for it." *As ready as we'll ever be.*

We talk for a few minutes about the research before I see Malachy's truck coming down the lane. I rush to meet them and relief washes over me when I see Finn. He looks great—tired, but like himself again.

He wraps me in a big bear hug and swings me in a circle. I laugh until he puts me down and I hand him a handmade card.

"Aw, Teag, that's cute," he says, holding back a laugh.

I look at the card with its barely recognizable drawing. "Brianna and Shannon dropped it off when they heard about the fire."

Finn's expression immediately changes. He holds the card tighter, and I glimpse the emotion swirling in his eyes. "Shannon is amazing."

"Yes, she is."

Tommy gets out of the truck, moving slower than Finn. Malachy supports him as he leads him to the cot set up in the mud room of the farmhouse.

"Come on, let's get you settled into your new room." I grab Finn's hand, pulling him to the sitting room.

Malachy and Nora set up a makeshift bed out of the couches, adorned with extra pillows and a soft patchwork quilt. We settle on the bed and Finn hands me his phone.

The image of the familiar Celtic barbs and snake sends a shock through me.

"I found it earlier today. Not much to do in the hospital, so I picked up a local newspaper and saw this article with the symbol. After reading it, I did some of my own research. I haven't had time to look too much into it, but it's bad, Teagan."

Scanning the page, my breath hitches. "A gang symbol."

Finn leans over. "Yeah, but before we jump to conclusions—"

"Jump to conclusions? It says right here that the garda have been trying to track down the Nathair gang for…well, their list of crimes is terribly long. They are considered armed and dangerous and shouldn't be trusted."

"Teagan, I know it looks bad, but maybe there's an explanation."

When I don't say anything, he slides his arms around my shoulders and whispers in my ear. "It's going to be okay." His eyes are protective, yet gentle. "We're in this together."

"I know." I smile at him. "And I don't know if I could do this alone. But Finn, it's not just Tommy or Ryan. It's the men from the pub who came to the farm, it's …" I close my eyes. "Seamus has a bracelet too."

"I know."

Before we can say more, Malachy and Nora join us.

"We know ye have the big presentation on Friday. Can we help with anything?" Malachy asks.

Finn and I exchange a look. While it's not on the top of our mind right now, we do want to run a few things by them. After I give them an overview of our presentation, we broach the tougher, practical aspects.

"We feel that by creating this program, not only will we help more people and animals, but we will allow the farm's legacy to live on," Finn says.

"We would need to find the right horses for the program first," I add. "And we think Sam and Gandalf would be perfect."

"That ol' menace?" Malachy exclaims.

"Yes, Gandalf. He has a way of understanding people's emotions." I give Malachy a pointed look.

Malachy grumbles something that I don't quite catch.

"Sam's gentleness is so encouraging. And Bilbo's size, being a Connemara pony, would be perfect for the younger kids. We think Aragorn and Arwen would be great eventually too, but they need a little more training."

"Good horses they are." Malachy nods.

"We would start with equine-assisted activities as the foundation, but develop a therapeutic riding program, including hippotherapy. I've been giving riding lessons for years, so it's natural while working with Shannon, but we want to go deeper with the riding, really targeting different muscle groups with exercises. We would need to find a few health and mental health professionals to help us develop these sessions for different needs, but all the research we've found on the impact of equine-assisted activities is very positive."

"What still needs doin'?" Malachy asks.

"Well, a lot. I've already signed up and started the process of becoming a therapeutic riding instructor. It's going to take a lot of work and many experiential hours, but I am so excited. I've already contacted an equine therapy program in Donegal, and they are happy to have us train with them and mentor our program. It's crazy that they're the closest center in Ireland. Three-and-a-half hours away is too far for most people and they aren't even accepting new clients now," I tell them. "Even if our proposal isn't selected, we still want to do this."

"Yeah, there's a real need for more centers. And with Teagan's riding experience and connection with horses, she's a natural." Finn sends me a smile. "Working with Shannon has been an amazing experience and seeing James and the potential for him, we know this program will help so many in the area."

"Ah, no doubt." Malachy has a look of resignation on his face.

"'Tis what God has been preparin' us for." Nora's tone is pleading.

"Nora," Malachy warns, "remember to keep ya head. The farm."

Nora begins to sob.

"Is the farm in that bad a shape?" Finn asks.

The sadness on their faces is all the answer we need.

"Afraid so," Malachy rubs his forehead. "We have a meetin' Friday afternoon at the bank."

Nora sobs louder.

"A foreclosure meetin'." Malachy presses on, despite his wife's audible sorrow. "If we don't sell to the bank, they'll have to foreclose on the farm."

Chapter Thirteen

"The Kavanaghs need to know about our suspicions."

Finn's right, and as much as I don't want to hurt them, they also need to know about Tommy's involvement with Nathair.

"Okay. Let's do it before breakfast."

We find Malachy and Nora at the table, drinking tea—like any other morning, except there's a tension in the air that didn't exist a few days ago.

We join them at the table and Finn draws a deep breath. "We need to tell you something."

I sit beside Nora. "We're concerned about Tommy."

Finn shifts in his seat. "Listen, I may be wrong about it all, but one night, I heard Tommy talking on the phone to what sounded like a debt collector. It sounded like he's in some trouble."

"Trouble?" Nora runs her fingers over the beads of her rosary.

"Financial trouble, which would explain the missing things around the farm and the money we know we saw in his drawer that day. We think it was there to pay off a debt."

"That's not all," I say as delicately as possible. "We also believe Tommy might be in the Nathair gang."

Nora lets out a small cry, crosses herself, and begins murmuring prayers.

"What makes ye say this?" Sadness swims in Malachy's eyes. No longer is there a refusal to believe Tommy would steal from them, but great apprehension.

Still feeling guilty for taking it, I hand the bracelet to Malachy. Slipping on his readers, he examines the symbol as he turns it around and around.

Finn moves next to the older man. "We thought it might be some Celtic symbol at first but couldn't find information on it anywhere. Then I saw a Northern Ireland news article in the hospital. The article had a photo of the symbol and its link to the Nathair gang."

Malachy removes his readers and rubs his eyes. "So it is." He gives a weak nod to Nora, who picks up the Bible never far from her side and begins flipping through the pages.

"Sorry, Malachy, we never meant to—" Finn begins.

"Stop right there. Ye did right by us."

The sound of beads falling on the table draws our attention back to Nora. She's standing hands on her hips. "We need to speak with Tommy. If he's in trouble, we can help him."

"Right ya are," Malachy agrees.

As the two of them walk out the door, I'm hit with the fact that they care more for Tommy than their own welfare. "He's likely stealing from them, but they want to help him," I say in disbelief as much as awe.

"He's family."

Brigid's Crossing is a special place, not because of the land or the possibility of finding a priceless emerald, but because it's a home built of love.

"They would rather help him than save the farm. I swear they're living saints."

"Teagan, look." Finn points to the Bible, open to Luke's gospel.

I pick it up and read the underlined verses. "To the person who strikes one cheek, offer the other one as well, and from the person who takes your cloak, do not withhold even your tunic. Give to everyone who asks of you, and from the one who takes what is yours do not demand it back. Do to others as you would have them do to you. For if you love those who love you, what credit is that to you?"

Finn taps the underlined verse further along the page. "'Be merciful, just as your Father is merciful.' I think what the Kavanaghs are teaching us is more valuable than any research experience could have been."

He wraps his arms around me, and I rest my head against his chest. "I think we're right where we're supposed to be."

"Me too," he whispers, then kisses the top of my head. "Teagan, I want you to know—"

The kitchen door flies open, shaking the teacups nestled on the silver platter.

"Tommy's gone," Nora cries, hand over her heart.

～

Malachy and Finn search for hours without any trace of Tommy. It's like he simply disappeared. Nora spends over an hour on the telephone calling what seems like everyone in Cloverdale and the surrounding area. My fingers itch to call Seamus and see if he knows anything, but then I remember that I was wrong about him. That revelation still hurts. I trusted Seamus…considered him a friend and someone I could rely on. To think he, Ryan, and Tommy have been in on this all along is too much. I think back to our conversations in the pub. Him encouraging us to find the emerald. Speaking about the Kavanaghs as beloved family.

I push down my rising anger and promise to not let anyone hurt these precious people again. They don't know about Seamus yet, and I don't know how to tell them. The way they've taken to Tommy's betrayal and disappearance, I'm afraid if they learn about Seamus, it will be too much. I consider the Kavanaghs my family now.

My stomach knots at the thought that our program will end before it's even had a chance to really begin. But even more than that, my heart aches at the devastation everything will bring to Malachy and Nora. I've been thinking about options that may allow them to keep the farm, but I keep coming up empty. The emerald, as far-fetched as it sounds, is our best option. But with the danger surrounding our treasure hunt, I don't know if we should even continue.

"Ready?" Nora ties her kerchief around her head.

I nod and follow her out the door.

Since no financial solutions can be found, and with Tommy missing, Nora asked me to go with her to St. Patrick's to light a candle. As we walk down the cobbled lane, I find myself praying for the first time in a long time.

God, I know I've been so focused on my own things recently that I haven't taken any time to talk to You. I'm sorry for pushing You into the background. I'm asking You now to help the Kavanaghs. Help us find Tommy, so he can get the help he needs. And if it's Your will, please let me find a way for them to keep Brigid's Crossing. And if You can find it in Your goodness to allow us the opportunity to start the equine-assisted therapy program, I promise to fulfill Your wish for it and share Your love with others.

"Holy ground this is," Nora says. "Did I ever tell ya the story of how Malachy and I started courtin'?"

"No, but I'd love to hear it."

"It was right here on this cobblestone lane. I had just turned eighteen and was on my way to St. Patrick's to pray for a very special intention. Malachy was walkin' Larry, the biggest Irish wolfhound ye've ever seen. The rain came out of nowhere, and I dropped my rosary in the mud. Rain was comin' down so hard I could barely see, so I was down on my hands and knees when this beast of a dog jumped on top of me." She laughs at the memory. "I screamed, but he started lickin' me, and my scream turned to laughter. Malachy, never the fastest runner, finally got to us and helped me up. Despite the rain slowin', we couldn't find the rosary."

She gets that far-off look in her eyes again. "He walked me to the church, and I found myself prayin' for two very special intentions that day. One was granted but the other was not. My Pa passed the next day from pneumonia. I was heartbroken but accepted it as God's will. At his wake, Malachy pulled me aside and put this rosary in my hand." She holds up her hand, worn wooden beads trailing down from her palm.

"Pa made that rosary, carved each bead, and tied each knot. 'Tis my dearest possession. The prayer deep in my heart was granted that day. And from that day onward, Malachy and I were a couple. We courted six months and Malachy proposed on this same lane." Nora stops and gestures around. "Right here."—

I look around, imagining them here in the pouring rain. A love story equal to my parents'. I've learned there are no two love stories exactly the same. Every couple has their own story—story that sings of their unique love.

"Do you think God meant for Malachy to find that rosary?"

"Indeed. Malachy gave me back my past, but also the promise of a future."

"You've made a life you love." My heart yearns for the same.

"I could'nt've made a greater one." Her eyes crinkle at the edges, lines worn deep. "I pray we can keep the farm, but if it's not God's will, then His will be done."

We walk on, the strength of Nora's faith making my steps feel steadier. What would it be like to have her faith? That confidence in God's will for her life? Even as I ask the question, I know it's possible for everyone. Nora has surrendered her life to God, and it's only in surrendering that peace can reside. *His will be done.* I know without a doubt that I haven't surrendered my will. I am so scared to lose control, my vision is narrow. I only see what I can do. God's vision is broader, and He knows what's best for us. As much as I understand that, I'm not sure how to completely surrender. St. Patrick's is just around the bend now, and I know my intentions for today, just as Nora did all those years ago.

"Nora, could you tell me about Eamon Kavanagh."

"Certainly, dear. What would ya like to know?"

"When we were at the Mahoney's, Caitlin mentioned that if we knew who Eamon was and what he treasured, then it might help us find the emerald."

"A strong woman, that Caitlin. I do believe she's on to somethin'. What can I say about Eamon?" She looks into the distance as if looking back in time. "A mighty character he was, but a heart of gold under that rugged exterior. Loved those horses."

"He bred racehorses, right?"

"Right you are. Some big winners too. Ah, he had his demons too, for sure and certain. A frequent visitor at the pubs, and the money was never around for long. But he had a way with the horses. I can't remember ever seein' him happier than groomin' the horses under the old willow tree. Only at those times can I remember him completely at peace. That was his treasure."

I picture the willow tree by the horse pasture, standing there so dignified and wise. Did I not picture myself reading under that tree when I arrived? That tree is special, there's no doubt. It's where Eamon felt peace.

We go into St. Patrick's and light a candle. Nora prays on her knees at the altar, while I take a seat in a pew a few rows back. This time my prayer is short. I don't worry about everything I want, but rather just pray. *God, You know my heart. Help me to know Yours. Lead me.*

A peace washes over me, and I know whatever the next day brings, I need must accept His will. As I sit there, soaking in the candlelit scene, my mind wanders to the farm. If Eamon chose to hide the map somewhere safe, where would it be? Eamon didn't feel that peace just from the willow tree but from what he was doing—grooming the horses.

And then it hits me. I know where he hid the map.

~

As night comes with no sign of Tommy, but a growing worry about the bank meeting, a heavy darkness settles on the farm. Even the stars appear to be hiding tonight. Our presentation time is early tomorrow morning, but how can we present the program proposal, knowing by the afternoon the farm will be gone, and our hope of the program along with it?

Needing to take this next step in the search alone, Finn and I wait for the Kavanaghs to go to bed before going to the stable.

"It's gotta be here." Frustration laces my tone. "Eamon was at peace with the horses. That's what Nora said. It's where he would keep the map, right?"

Finn nods, as a touch of sympathy shines in his eyes. "We just have to keep looking. Let's think— is there anything with special meaning to him in here?"

"Let's groom the horses."

"Okay. Not exactly what I was saying."

"He loved grooming the horses, so let's put ourselves in his position. See what he saw, hear what he heard. That may lead us to the answer."

Finn shrugs. "Worth a try."

We walk Sam out of his stall and hook the cross ties to his halter. Gandalf hangs his head over the stall door and whinnies. We laugh at his obvious need for attention. Over the past few weeks, Gandalf has proven himself more than just a nuisance—he's a horse with a huge heart. He craves attention and acts out to get it.

"You're a cuddle bug, aren't you?" I rub a hand along his neck, and he leans into it. "You wanna get groomed too?"

Gandalf answers with a loud snort.

"Okay, I hear you," I tell him.

Finn laughs behind us.

"You okay with Sam while I groom Gandalf?" I ask him.

Finn wraps his arms around my waist and kisses my cheek. "Sure. I don't think he'd have it any other way."

After I secure Gandalf to the second set of cross ties, we fall into a steady rhythm. I rub the curry comb in circular motions across the animal's body, focusing on his withers and back. Loose hair settles in clumps on his back. Taking a dandy brush, I use flicking movements to brush the hair off. Then I run a soft brush over his body. Gandalf's head hangs and his eyelids droop. His grey coat shines from the soft goat hair bristles.

I rest my head against his smooth shoulder. The strength and power of his muscles twitch under my weight. I'm always amazed that a powerful sixteen-hundred-pound animal like Gandalf feels the tiny bite of a fly. Under all that strength and power is a unique gentleness.

Gandalf lifts his front leg to swat at a circling fly. When his hoof touches the ground a clump of dried mud falls.

"Oh, I forgot to clean your hooves."

Shaking my head at my own forgetfulness, I search the grooming tote for a hoof pick.

Lifting his front leg to a ninety-degree angle, I rest his hoof on my thigh. Gripping the pick by the rubber, I gently scrape away caked-on mud from the sides and grooves. I'm careful not to nick the center V-shaped frog, which acts as a shock absorber and protects the circulation. As I inspect the now-clean hoof, Malachy's words flash through my mind.

The tools.

"Finn!"

Gandalf startles at my voice. "Sorry, boy. I promise I'll finish your hooves later." I unhook the crossties and put him back into the stall as his tail flicks in annoyance.

"What's going on?" Finn asks. Sam is already back in his stall, comfortably munching hay.

"The tools." I emphasize each word.

Finn's brows furrow. "What tools?"

"Eamon's tools. Malachy and Nora told us about them. The ones believed to be forged in St. Brigid's school for metal works."

"The Kavanaghs said they are in the tack room." Realization dawns in Finn's eyes.

"And they haven't seen them since Eamon passed away, so the map could be there, and they would've never known."

Hurrying to the tack room, my heart pounds in my chest. "We are so close. I can feel it."

Excitement shines in Finn's eyes.

As I slide around a box of old lead ropes in the corner, my shoe catches on a curved nail jutting out of a loose floorboard.

"Finn, look."

We kneel on the floor, pushing old boxes out of the way.

"These boxes must've been here for ages." Finn pushes the last of them to the side wall.

"Maybe they were hiding something?"

"Only one way to find out."

We begin pulling at the loose floorboard until it creaks and snaps up. Dirt covers the area until it dips to one side, the curve of a hole. Peering into the dark gap, we see an outline of a rounded object standing out from the hole.

"Should I reach in?" I ask tentatively.

"Let's try to get another board up."

"But if it's not down there, how are we going to explain tearing up the floor?"

"The Kavanaghs will understand. Anyway, why is there a hole under there if not to hide something?"

Makes sense. Eamon wouldn't have wanted any chance of those tools being stolen. But my sensible mind is shouting to check first. Scanning the room, I spot a small black object.

"Flashlight!"

Finn grabs it and lies on the ground, shining the light into a space between the boards. "Looks like a bucket of some kind."

"Can you see what's in it?"

"No, just the side. Real dirty though. Been down there a long time."

"Ok, let's do it."

Finn begins tearing the neighboring boards up.

"Maybe you missed your calling. You're looking like quite the carpenter right now."

Finn laughs. "Yeah, well usually carpenters are building things, not tearing them apart."

"Technicalities." I give him a little shove.

The missing boards reveal a small black bucket snug within the surrounding hole. A crack runs down one side of the pail while the handle is broken in the center, leaving two loose fragments of metal.

A horseshoe lies on top of a pile of similarly rusted tools. A hammer, nippers, rasps, and a hoof knife.

"I would think they'd be more rusted than they are," I whisper, in awe of the craftmanship.

"They must've been cared for before they were buried."

An image of a long line of Kavanaghs sitting in the tack room, cleaning and polishing the metal comes to mind. These tools are a part of the Kavanagh family treasure.

"Teagan." Finn's tone startles me from my thoughts. His mouth is open, disbelief evident on his face.

I follow his gaze. A rolled, weathered scroll lays at the bottom of the bucket. "The map."

Finn extracts the paper and places it in my hand. The paper is cold and dusty. Its delicate edges are fraying, and it feels thin as my thumb slides over the length of the scroll, bumping at the twine twisted around the center. I pull the thin string with care, allowing the paper to stretch and unroll the edges one tiny movement at a time.

Scattered black ink lines the paper, with a red X in the middle.

"I can't believe it," Finn says with a laugh.

"I know. Wait till we show the Kavanaghs."

"We can't do anything now, in this darkness. We'll wait until tomorrow after our presentation. They're going to need their asleep for the adventure in store for us tomorrow."

Chapter Fourteen

The car beeps for a third time as Ronan calls out the window.

"Teagan, we need to leave if we're going to make the presentation."

Our research presentation is scheduled for eight o'clock at Emerald Isle, but we're running out of time. I sprint toward the truck.

"We need to go to the bank." I jump into the front seat. "What?"

"The Kavanaghs are gone. The meeting was moved up to this morning and they're already on their way."

It takes a minute for this information to settle before Finn begins driving down the lane in the direction of the town.

"Do you have it with you?"

I pull the faded weathered paper out of my bag and open it to reveal the detailed sketch.

"Teagan, you know if we go by the bank, we're going to miss our presentation." Finn sends me a cautious glance.

"I know. Some things are more important. If we get this to the Kavanaghs in time, then we can find the emerald and it could save the farm." Adrenaline has me breathing heavily in anticipation of the hunt ahead.

"Yeah. That would be amazing. But Teagan, there's still a chance that we won't find the emerald. Anything could have happened between when this map was drawn and now. It could all be for nothing."

"I know, but even if we never find it, we have to try. Brigid's Crossing is too important."

"And it's worth the risk?"

"Yes! But if you don't want to—"

Finn presses the accelerator. "Let's go."

~

"Don't sell! Don't sell!" I run past the secretary and burst into the meeting room, waving the map like a victory flag. "Don't sell."

Five sets of eyes stare at me, and I take a few deep breaths.

"Good heavens, what's the matter, dear?" Nora hurries to me and gently rubs my back.

"We found it," Finn says from behind me. Leaning down, he whispers into my ear, "You should have tried out for track and field in high school."

I laugh, as his breathing is a great deal more labored than mine.

"Found what?" A man in a crip black suit and green bow tie sits behind an ancient typewriter, a pipe hanging out of his mouth.

I turn to Nora. "We found the map."

Malachy jumps from his seat and joins us. Tears well in his eyes as he looks at it. "Ye found it?" he says, shaking his head in disbelief. "Where?"

"When Nora and I went to St Patrick's yesterday, she told me how she's never seen Eamon happier than when he groomed the horses under the old willow tree, and I remember you guys telling us about the ancient farrier tools in the tack room. We went to look last night, and the map was just lying there, right on top of the tools. I didn't want to say anything and get your hopes up in case I was wrong."

"Them ol' tools. Of course," Malachy says. "Why we never thought of it, I'll never know."

"Malachy, our prayers have been answered." Nora kisses the gold crucifix around her neck. "Told ya He wouldn't leave us forlorn."

"Indeed."

"Malachy," the green-bow-tied man says, "you can't be talkin' about that emerald."

"Sure am, Mac. Give me a wee bit of time. We're goin' to save the farm."

Mac raises his eyebrows before a large grin spreads across his face. "Be off with ye! And Malachy, I hope ya find ye're treasure."

Treasure.

This time the words are like an arrow pointing to the farm.

~

We count thirty steps and dig into the soft, wet ground. Forty minutes and quite a few holes later, we've found nothing.

"Oh, dear," Nora sighs.

"Ah, a good try," Malachy agrees, both seeming to accept defeat.

"We can't give up yet." Finn's brows scrunch in thought. "What are we missing? If only we knew how deep…or maybe our measurements are off."

Little James Mahoney's words come back to me. "Or maybe it's not buried in the *ground*."

Recognition crosses Finn's face before a smile begins to grow.

"The willow," we say together, glancing up at the tree towering over us.

"Be careful with ya," Nora pleads as Finn gives me a lift and I climb onto the mid-section, steadying myself on a large branch. "Don't need no broken bones now."

I smile at her motherly devotion. My heart skips a beat at the sight of the wooden St. Brigid's cross nailed into a crevice of the old tree.

"A St. Brigid's cross," I call down.

Finn's grin widens, and Nora makes the Sign of the Cross.

"Go 'head, lassie!" Malachy bellows, pure joy streaming on each word.

I gently tug the wood and nails, removing each nail without too much damage to the wood. With a final pop, the cross in my hand reveals a hole in the trunk. I reach in, curving my fingers around a chest about the size of a ring box.

A rectangle of gold with a hinged lid rests in my palm. A delicate leafy design is etched around the border. The bottom is engraved with the name Diaz. Running my finger over the name, I think about the family and their kindness. Slipping it into my jacket pocket, I climb down the old tree.

"You should do the honors." I hand Malachy the chest.

He holds it like the precious treasure it is.

"Stop right there!" a woman's voice rings out.

A familiar figure stalks toward us, her hips swaying over the rocky terrain. Matching her stride for stride, Ryan holds a gun pointed straight at us, a wicked snarl on his face. Behind him a shadow sways back and forth.

"Fiona?" Nora asks. "What are ya doing here?"

Fiona's eyes lock on the chest. Fiery tendrils frame her face, making her look more like a demonic enchantress than a woman. Standing in front of Malachy, she reaches for the chest.

"I wouldn't do that," Ryan drawls when Malachy pulls away. He raises his hand and points the gun directly at Malachy's forehead. A cry escapes Nora's lips.

"Give it to me!" Fiona yells, flames shooting from her eyes.

Hands trembling, the elderly man hands her the chest, a silent plea in his eyes.

Her lips, painted red like blood from a predator's feast, curve into a wicked grin. A glance at Finn reveals he's managed to call emergency services without being noticed.

"Finally." She slowly opens the lid of the chest and whimpers. "Where is it?"

"It's not there," I whisper to Finn, unable to believe what's happening.

"The chest is empty!" Fiona screams.

We all step back, including Ryan. It's then that the figure behind him finally steps forward.

Tommy.

At the sight of him, Malachy's hand goes to his chest, and he slowly drifts to the ground, leaning against the tree trunk. Tommy's face is bruised, his eyes swollen, and blood drips from the corner of his mouth.

Fiona throws the chest against the trunk of the tree, only inches from Malachy. Falling to the ground, she crawls to the broken chest, clawing at it like a feral cat. "No, no, no, no."

If Fiona had any sanity left, it's gone now. She pulls a gun from the holster around her waist and aims it at Malachy's chest. "Where is it? I won't be askin' again." Keeping her gaze on our little group, she finds the safety with her thumb and pulls it back.

"Please, no. You can take whatever ya want." Tears rain down Nora's cheeks as she pleads with the younger woman. "Just don't take my Malachy."

Fiona doesn't spare her a glance. Her finger inches closer and closer to the trigger. "Where is it?"

Malachy stares at her, a stunned expression frozen in place. "I don't have the faintest idea," he finally says, and slumps further to the ground.

"We need to get outta here," Finn murmurs to me.

"How?"

"A distraction."

"What?" I look around desperately, and then I see him. "We don't need to do anything."

"What?"

I nod to the field not even thirty feet away. The field Finn and I first encountered all those weeks ago. Finn's lips begin to curl as he watches Gandalf kick the last of the boards off the fence before charging right at us.

The sound of a gunshot echoes in my ears. Finn sweeps me into his arms and tucks me safely under him on the ground. We lie there as time seems to stand still.

When the ringing finally subsides, I slowly open my eyes.

"Nora!" I gasp, scrambling to stand up. She's leaning over a man's body, red blood pooling in her hands.

Crouching next to her, I put an arm around her shoulders and look into Tommy's pale face, withered in pain.

"We'll get ye good 'n fit, lad." On Tommy's other side, Malachy's face is ashen, a stream of blood running down his face.

"Where was he shot?" Finn asks.

"Stomach. Bugger jumped right in front of me."

Nora's cries are muffled as an ambulance pulls into the drive. EMTs rush to the scene and a couple of garda exit their vehicles.

I help Nora stand, and the EMTs take over, applying pressure to Tommy's wound and getting him ready for transport.

"He'll be at the hospital in no time." I hope my encouraging words for Nora are true.

"Where are Fiona and Ryan?" I ask Finn.

He points to the old shed about fifty yards from the willow tree.

"Come out with ye hands up!" a garda yells.

"Can't go anywhere with that beast out there!" Fiona shouts back.

The garda exchanges a look with Malachy.

"Right." Gandalf nuzzles Malachy as he leads him back to the field. The garda walk Fiona in handcuffs toward the patty wagon, but then stop suddenly as she calls our way.

"We'll get ya again!"

"Enough with ya," the burly garda says, and they continue to the wagon. "She'd take the pennies from a dead man's eyes."

Fiona hisses at him before being strapped in behind the bars of the wagon. Turning to us, pure hatred fills her eyes.

⁓

After the last of the search parties return, it appears Ryan escaped without a trace. A larger manhunt has begun, but I get a feeling from the garda that he has connections all over Ireland and there's a good likelihood he won't be found any time soon. The thought that he's out there somewhere, biding his time, sends a chill down my spine.

I lean back into the loveseat and look around the sitting room, memories of our first day here flashing through my mind. We're in the same spots, but how different we all are from that day. Finn's bedding is folded neatly on the side of the sofa, a reminder of recent events. To think we were so close to saving the farm and then failed. "It's a shame the emerald wasn't there. I really believed it would save the farm. To come so close and lose it all is heartbreaking."

"Don't lose hope just yet, lass." A glint sparkles in Malachy's eyes. He pulls a crumpled piece of paper out of his pocket.

"Malachy, good heavens. What is this?" Nora asks, crossing herself.

""'Tis a note from Da. It was stickin' out of the linin' of that little chest. Would've never seen it if not for Fiona rippin' it up. That ol' bugger was smarter than he ever got credit for."

Nora walks to his side, drapes an arm over his shoulder and reads the note aloud.

To give all you have to help another is where you'll find true treasure. The right person will find this stone and use it for good. And may good fortune and love be with you all the days of your life.

"The emerald was never in the chest," I say in disbelief. "He hid it somewhere else. But where?"

Malachy and Nora look at each other, a full conversation in a single look.

"St. Brigid's Cross," they say together, and we all hurry to the stable.

Finn pulls a ladder around and helps steady it while Malachy climbs to the top. He pulls out the nail, and gently passes the cross to Nora. She carefully unfolds the willow branches, each one like the whisper of a silent prayer. Finally, at the last twist, her hands go still. She hands the cross back to Malachy. "Ya do it."

"We do it together."

Just as they've done throughout their marriage, they work together until the last set of twigs untangle to reveal a gem more precious than any I've ever seen.

Chapter Fifteen

On the way to the bank the next day, we stop by the hospital to visit Tommy.

He looks at the floor, unable to meet our eyes. "I was trapped and never wanted you guys involved in any of this."

My heart pounds. "Tommy, you should have been honest with us. We could've helped you. And Seamus."

"Seamus? What about Seamus?"

"Isn't he in Nathair with you?"

"Seamus? In Nathair?" He gives a painful laugh. "Seamus would never be part of Nathair."

He's innocent.

"Seamus?" Nora asks. "What about Seamus?"

"Why did you get involved with them to begin with?" Finn veers the conversation away from the Kavanaghs' beloved nephew.

"I got into some trouble in Limerick and then Dublin. Gambling mostly, but some drugs too. I borrowed money from the wrong people and couldn't get myself out of the hole. That's where I met Ryan. He offered to pay off all my debts if I could get a job on the farm and find out what I could about the emerald. I had to report in weekly with him. Then, when he didn't think I was doing my job good enough, he got the job at the pub, and that's when I met Fiona. She scared me from the start. Ryan was tough, but there was something pure evil about Fiona."

"That's why she asked us to be in the scholar's program," Nora whispers.

Tommy nods, eyes to the floor. "A means to an end. That's why I ran. I thought if I left, they would come after me and leave ya'll alone." He shakes his head. "I should have known better. There was only one thing on their minds."

"Ya'll be home soon enough."

Tommy looks at me. "Teagan, you think the horses will ever trust me again?"

"Horses have a way of understanding the true nature of a person. And they know you, Tommy."

"I wish I could go back and—"

"No good worrying about the past," Malachy says.

"Malachy, Nora, I'm so sorry." His voice breaks.

"Now, now, no need for that. Everyone deserves a second chance. We're goin' to get through this together." Nora squeezes his hand. "Ye're a fine young lad."

Finn and I leave to allow the couple time alone with Tommy.

"I talked to Malachy earlier and looks like he's trying to get Tommy out on probation under his care," Finn tells me once we're seated in the waiting room. "He's not the one they want. They're after Ryan and the leaders of Nathair. As long as Tommy cooperates, he will probably get off easy."

"Tommy found his place at Brigid's Crossing. Malachy and Nora will rescue him, like the horses."

Finn slides his arm around me and pulls me close. "We all found something at Brigid's Crossing." He kisses the top of my head.

"For once, you'll get no argument from me," I mumble into his chest as my eyes grow heavy and gradually close.

I awake to the sound of Malachy and Nora's voices as they join Finn and me.

"Who's ready to go to the bank?" Malachy asks, a big grin on his face.

I still can't believe he's walking around with a fifteen-carat emerald in his pocket. I may have held my breath the entire walk from the hospital.

As we watch the Kavanaghs walk up the bank steps, their hands intertwined, I know everything will be okay. The farm will survive and live on through the generations. The Kavanaghs may not have had any children, but they've grown a strong family in Cloverdale. And the farm and their legacy will endure.

"I can't believe they've offered to give us the money to start the program at Brigid's Crossing. I just don't know how we're going to do it without Emerald Isle and the research support."

Finn squeezes my hand. "Come with me to St. Patrick's. I want to show you something."

I'm not sure what St. Patrick's has to do with our research, but I'm happy to follow Finn. "Lead the way."

As we walk down the cobblestones to the old church, I'm reminded of Nora and Malachy's fateful day on the cobblestone lane.

Finn pulls the heavy door open and the fragrant aroma of incense floats from the sanctuary. He stops in front of one of the stained-glass windows in the vestibule. This one I haven't noticed before. It's a depiction of the Irish countryside. An old man and a young boy are in the forefront, a horse standing next to them. The horse's head is tilted down to the boy as he reaches a hand up to stroke its muzzle. As the sun shines through the window, a golden halo forms around the three. My breath catches at the resemblance to James and Hugo.

"God was leading us to this life all along," Finn whispers.

"It's what we're meant to do…I feel it." Tears fill my eyes. "But it's too late now. We missed our presentation."

"About that," Finn interrupts. "I spoke with the university and, given the circumstances, they have agreed to meet with us and allow us to do the presentation. They said they need to talk to the board, and they can't promise anything. So, if you still want to do it, we have a chance." He checks his watch. "But we need to leave now."

Taking one last look at the scene shining bright in front of me, I smile at Finn. "We have to try."

—

"Every person deserves to be treated with dignity and respect. Animals, horses in particular, can show this compassion to those who sometimes lack it in their lives. They allow us to open up without the fear of judgment or condemnation from others. In an animal's eyes, they're not seeing us the way people look at each other—analyzing and adding up the facts on our appearance. Animals look at our hearts. That's what they see. And they reflect this in their actions. This is the way horses act as a mirror, letting us know how we're feeling when we may not even know. They show us what we're radiating to others and can then help us transfer our actions to human relationships.

"Animals give us a second chance in a world where second chances are often dismissed. They present the open door that is closed in the faces of those with special needs. And once they walk through the door, the whole world looks different. It's no longer a place of judgment and ridicule, but a place where love exists. And when we experience love," I look at Finn, "that love never leaves us. It travels with us and becomes a part of us so that every interaction we have after that encounter is seen in a new way."

Finn smiles at me as we face four Emerald Isle board members. "There are obstacles that stand in all our paths.

These obstacles can seem daunting, and we can feel power-less in the midst of them. But with the right support, we can persevere and overcome these roadblocks, leading to a happier and healthier life. Data shows that increased positive human interactions follow equine-assisted activities."

I hand out the article and our summary to the board as I talk. "Our first study looks at the effects of therapeutic riding on the development of children with autism. Evaluation of strides served as assessments for coordination of movement. Twenty-six students—twenty boys and twenty girls of special needs—participated in therapeutic riding. The research included a non-riding control group. The skills were measured using the Pedagogical Analysis and Curriculum (PAC) test and the Gait Cycle Analysis, including time-series analysis of gait cycle and the measurement of joint angles in each plane of movement. Significant differences were found in the riding group as compared to the non-riding group. They suggest that therapeutic riding should be considered as a form of additional support for children with autism, and possibly for any needing physical rehabilitation."

Finn holds up another stack of papers. "These are many more examples of scholarly articles providing the same analysis and result. Therapeutic riding needs to be further explored to provide the scientific backing so crucial for its treatment to be more widespread."

I chime back in. "It is the 'blessing of the horses,' as my parents always said. They're both equine veterinarians, so I grew up with horses. They founded a practice and rescue farm back in the US, and I was lucky enough to see firsthand the way these amazing animals can change lives. We have the opportunity to build a partnership with horses to teach others about the dignity of each person and their innate value in society. Everyone is loved just for themselves. When they feel this love, the difference in their attitude and spirit shows in every aspect of their lives."

Finn steps forward. "We want our program to not only be one of scientific endeavor, worthy of the most stringent regulations and data collection, but also a healing path for the person as a whole—body, mind, heart, and soul. St. John Paul II, wrote in *Fides et ratio*, 'Faith and reason are like two wings on which the human spirit rises to the contemplation of truth; and God has placed in the human heart a desire to know the truth—in a word, to know himself—so that, by knowing and loving God, men and women may also come to the fullness of truth about themselves.'"

He gestures to the board members. "When we talk about faith and reason, we are not just saying reason is the ability to think clearly and come to the correct answers to scientific problems, but rather an opportunity to increase in wisdom. Reason should be united with wisdom. Without wisdom, advancements in science are just numbers and facts. But we know that science is more than just numbers and facts, it's about life."

I move to stand beside Finn as he continues. "We know this is different from other science research proposals." The looks on their faces confirm this statement to be completely true. "We know we're going outside the bounds with this. But we truly believe that we need to push those boundaries to practice the type of science that will truly change the world for the better. We don't just want a good grade or even a spot in this program, as much as we would love one." A murmur of laughter circles the room. "We know we may not be able to change the whole world, but with our research, we hope to change the world for those that need it the most."

"And that's what our research is all about," Finn continues. "Having a positive effect on the lives of people through nurturing the human-animal bond. A bond that has unparalleled possibilities, but one that has not been given the chance to fully make a difference in the scientific community."

Passion radiates from Finn's every word. He is displaying the same passion I fell in love with during those first chemistry labs, listening to his thoughts and wonderings about the topic we were studying. Finn has a mind for science and a passionate heart for research. I can't imagine a better partner to have, in school and in life.

"We hope you will give us the chance to bring equine-assisted activities to the forefront of scientific discovery."

There's a moment of silence before one gentleman looks up from his notes. "And what would ye're program be called?"

It occurs to me that we never discussed a name. I look at Finn and see the love in his eyes, so familiar yet so very new. "Second Chances."

~

"How long do you think they'll be?" I ask Finn, as we sit on a narrow bench in the hallway. They've been discussing our presentation for the last fifteen minutes.

"Maybe it's a good thing," he says with a shrug.

"It's funny. I should be a nervous wreck, but I'm not. We did everything we could. I know this is the research we're being called to, and with that comes a sense of peace. It will happen. Maybe not today, but He'll find a way if it is His will."

"I couldn't agree more."

Just as he kisses me the door opens.

"Teagan and Finn, please join us."

After we're seated, the board members exchange glances before Mr. Banwell clears his throat.

"We can say, in all honesty, that this is the most unique and thought-provokin' research proposal we have yet seen. It's clear this is a little-investigated area in science and one we can benefit explorin'."

"And," Mrs. Dolan smiles, "we all know how powerful the bond can be between a person and an animal. We see it in our own lives. The dogs, cats, bunnies, sheep, you name it. But horses have always held a special place in the hearts of the Irish people."

"Right ya are," Mr. Banwell agrees. "We love the proposal. Best proposal of the program."

My heart leaps in my chest.

"But we already awarded the prize to another group."

The words hit me like a hammer. "Okay." I respond quickly, determined not to give way to the tears stinging my eyes. "We understand."

"However...because of the situation involvin'"—the board members exchange a pointed look— "your mentor, we are willin' to offer you a place in our program."

I let out a little cry. *We have a spot!*

He raises a hand. "There's one stipulation. While we can let you into the program, our grant money will not cover both projects, so ye'll need to come up with additional fundin' for yours."

Finn smiles at me before turning back to the board. "I don't think that will be a problem."

After a quick call to the Kavanaghs and the assurance of their financial backing for our project, we are officially welcomed into student research positions at Emerald Isle.

"It feels like a dream," I tell Kayleigh and Ashling over the phone. They'll leave for the airport in a few minutes and will be here tomorrow morning. I cannot wait to see them and my parents. So much has happened in the past weeks that nothing feels the same anymore.

"I'm so proud of you. I never doubted you'd make it for a minute. And I still can't believe that after all this time you and Finn are finally together," Kayleigh says.

"Yes, we are expecting the president to call with his warmest wishes for your relationship any minute."

"Ashling, don't worry. You will find your true love too."

"Kayleigh, if you mention the word love one more time this summer—"

"Okay, you two, we'll have plenty of time to talk tomorrow. I just wanted to tell you the news before you leave."

"Congrats, Teag. I have no doubt you will win your Nobel prize before you graduate." This time there's genuine pride in Ashling's voice.

"Thanks, Ashling. But, honestly, as long as our program helps people, that's the only prize I need. Love you guys. Safe travels!"

After we hang up, I know the words are true.

I have found my treasure.

Chapter Sixteen

Later that evening, Finn and I sit on the porch swing, alone at last. Gratitude fills my heart. I am here with the most amazing guy, our whole future ahead of us. I have fantasized about my parents' romance for so long that I lost track of my own path. My relationship with Finn may not develop the same as theirs, but ours is just as beautiful. We all have a path to travel, and only when we follow the one God has set out for us do we find peace.

"I love the idea that the emerald is funding our research. It's like that long-lost jewel lives on in the program."

"Like the Diaz family is a part of it too."

"Absolutely."

I love how he just gets me. He always has, and now we can finally see where it leads.

"Antonella was thrilled when I told her about the program," I tell him. "Like she's as invested as we are."

"I think she is, in a way. Malachy was telling me that Antonella and Nora were talking about her coming back to live on the farm for a little while, working with Nora and learning more about her grandparents. He said she could be here as early as next month."

"It's amazing the way things work out. I bet she never in a million years thought she would be living in Ireland."

"Well, that makes two of us then. And I think Tommy is more than happy to have Antonella around."

I laugh, thinking back to his behavior when she was here. "I hope he finds his ability to speak around her."

Finn tightens his arm around me. "He'll get there, it just may take him a little while." His fingertips brush my cheek.

"Some things are worth waiting for," I whisper back.

We sit in comfortable silence until my phone rings. An unknown Ireland phone number blinks on the screen.

"Hello?"

"Is this Teagan O'Reilly?"

"Yes."

"Caitlin Doherty from Donegal Equine Therapy."

I click the speaker button so Finn can hear.

"Hi, Ms. Doherty. It's so nice to hear from you."

"Please call me Caitlin. Colin Banwell from Emerald Isle contacted me about ye're research proposal."

"Oh, how kind of him."

There's a brief silence before she replies. "Aye. He's…a persuasive man. Anyway, I'd love to offer ye a partnership with Donegal. A mentorship of sorts."

"We'd love that," I tell her with mounting enthusiasm. "We really appreciate it. I'm so glad Mr. Banwell got in touch. This will be great."

Another silence. "Aye. Mr. Banwell has big plans…I know ye'll be in the US for a couple weeks, but when you return, I'll be in touch."

"Thank you so much. We look forward to working with you."

"Aye. We'll speak soon."

After ending the call, I turn to Finn. His expression is one of worry. "Did she sound kind of hesitant to you?"

"No, she sounds nice. And she said Mr. Banwell has big plans. I didn't realize we made such an impression during our presentation."

Finn looks lost in thought, causing questions to swirl in my mind. "Why? Do you think it was odd?"

After a moment, he shakes his head. "Not exactly. Maybe I'm just being overly paranoid after everything's that's happened."

"Well, that's easy to understand. The past few weeks have been an adventure, to say the least."

He laughs. "Yeah, still can't believe how everything went down."

"I know. I mean, we were in a full-out treasure hunt, with a gang, looking for a lost emerald. Crazy."

"Well, can't wait to see what this next year brings."

Thoughts of the future fill my mind as we watch the rain fall.

~

The next day, Seamus joins us at the farm. He was shocked to learn about the recent events and took a few days off to stay at the farm and help Malachy and Nora with their business.

"Can't believe it," he says for about the hundredth time. "Ya think ya know someone…but he turns out to be a dope."

Seamus is taking the news of Ryan's involvement hard. I get it but wish he wouldn't blame himself.

"Seamus, you couldn't have known what was going on," I assure him.

"I trusted the eegit," he mumbles. "He'd skin a flea for a halfpenny."

Hurt shines in his eyes. Seamus is a true friend, and Ryan broke his trust. A wave of guilt washes over me as I wonder how I could've ever thought he was in on their plan. Even

Tommy had known this guy would never be a part of the Nathair gang. How was I so blind?

"I know, and that speaks of how great of a guy you are."

He waves this off. The bracelet is noticeably gone from his wrist.

"Seamus, where's your bracelet?" I ask tentatively.

"Ah, threw it in the Dublin Bay, I did."

At my confused look, he continues. "Ryan gave it to me. Talkin' all about brotherhood and bullock." He waves his hand. "He's not the kind of brother I want, so into the sea with it."

I laugh at his straightforward solution, happy to be able to relax around him again.

"I have no words. An Irish man with no words. What kind of blarney is that?" Seamus throws his hands up in the air.

I glance at my watch. *No words?* We've been at the kitchen table for over an hour rehashing everything. I stifle my grin and try to think of a way to help Seamus understand he's not to blame.

"Well, what about me and Finn? We trusted Fiona and she turned out to be insane. Literally insane."

It's Seamus' turn to laugh. "Aye, right ya are. She went mental all right."

"Yes, completely. Like out-of-a-horror-movie crazy. But Finn and I can't blame ourselves for that. We couldn't have known what she was planning. We couldn't control the choices she made." I pause and speak softly. "Just like you couldn't have known about Ryan or his choices."

He nods, understanding dawning in his eyes. "I hear ya, Teagan."

"We have so much to look forward to, we can't get stuck in the past. We need to learn from those experiences, but we also need to move on. I mean, we're getting ready to start *Second Chances*, and that's going to be amazing."

Earlier in the day, Finn and I spoke with Seamus about helping out with the program. He's good with the business end of things and we could use the help. He's been running *Rocky Shore Fishing*, the company he founded, for a couple years and has great experience to share. He also has his experience at O'Callahan's and their partnership with his company. Even more than his ability to help on the business side, we want him to be a part of the program because he's family.

"Right," Seamus says, a full smile forming now. "And I'll help in any way I can."

"I know you will. How's the fishing business going these days?"

"Grand. Never thought it would take off the way it has. Might be givin' my notice in the pub soon."

"Really? To focus on your fishing?"

"Aye. Been a dream of mine since I was a lad. Ya and Finn need to see the boat one day."

"We'd love that. Do you have a name for it?"

"All sailors have a name for their boats. Mine is *Crossways*."

"Aren't they supposed to be named after a woman?"

"No woman to name her after. But Yeats carried me through many rough patches."

"You like W.B. Yeats?"

"Ah, go on with ya, Teagan. The Irish are poets! It runs in our blood."

"Okay, sorry," I say, laughing. "I just never pictured you reading poetry."

"Write some too."

"No way!"

"Ya don't have to look so surprised!"

"It's just…well, you and my sister, Kayleigh, would really hit it off."

"Is that so? I'm quite the catch, ya know."

"Quite," I reply with a grin, matchmaking schemes already forming in my mind. "Seriously, that's really neat about the poetry, Seamus. So, why *Crossways?*"

"'Tis the name of Yeats' first collection of poetry. '*The salmon-falls, the mackerel-crowded seas, fish, flesh, or fowl, commend all summer long. Whatever is begotten, born, and dies. Caught in that sensual music all neglect. Monuments of unagein' intellect.*' It helped me through my parents passin'." Seamus pauses before continuing. "I could see myself in the poem. I was a young lad with an old soul."

"That's beautiful."

"Aye, well, didn't write it, just connected with it. Then, took an evenin' class in Irish literature at the university and I was hooked. Even got the job at the pub through poetry."

My mouth drops open. "How?"

"See, they hold a poetry readin' the first Friday of the month. I was there when Mr. O'Callahan was lookin' for help. Hired me on the spot, right after hearin' me read."

"What did you read?"

"Now that's for another day," Seamus says with a wink.

I sigh. "Okay. I'll have to check out the Irish literature course at Emerald Isle."

"Grand idea. Ya won't regret it. And I hear ya mates won the research spots."

"Yes! Zoey and Kyle won with their proposal and will be at Emerald Isle too. It's perfect. Zoey and I can't wait to be roommates again. And Finn and Kyle are excited too. It worked out better than we could've ever hoped. Almost seems too good to be true that all four of us are in the program."

"Ah, but it is true. That ol' Irish luck. Now when do I get to meet this American family of yours?"

As if on cue, their taxi pulls into the drive. A door opens and Kayleigh steps out, looking gorgeous in a green cotton dress, white jean jacket, and leather sandals. Her hair is loose, curly tendrils flowing down her back.

"Who is that?"

Seamus stands at the window, mouth agape, and a I can't hold back a laugh. This is going to be interesting.

Chapter Seventeen

"You've found your way." Mom hands me a cup of tea as my sisters' laughter bubbles in the background.

"I came to Ireland thinking everything would be magical. The Irish tradition for magic and tales was so intriguing, but things don't have to have powers to be special. There are miracles every day—we just need to look for them."

"Your time here has been so good for you. I've never seen you so happy or relaxed. It's nice to see."

"Yeah, I guess there's a contentment that comes with knowing you're where you're supposed to be, doing what you're called to do. Before this summer, I was anxious about so many things. I had everything planned, but those plans went flying out the window when I got to the airport."

We laugh at the memory.

"Is Finn really okay with his parents not being here? I can't image how demanding Admiral Connelly's job must be for him to miss this."

"Yeah," I tell her with a sigh. I think I can imagine where the admiral's priority lies. "I think he's used to it. I wish they could've come too, but it'll be nice having him traveling with us. And his mom is meeting him at the airport, so that's good."

"True. And I won't mind getting to know the boy who's stolen my girl's heart twice now."

"Well, I don't know about stolen. I'd say I've given it away freely, both times." I'm still in awe of God's timing in my life. "Antonella once said that her grandmother told her that when you look into the emerald you see your heart's wish."

"I can't wait to meet this Antonella. She seems like a wonderful girl, and what a strong nature in coming to Ireland and leaving everything behind."

"She's not leaving it all behind, Mom. She's bringing it with her."

My mom looks at me in a way I've never seen before. A look that goes beyond pride to a new level of respect. "And what did you see in the emerald?"

How to explain what I saw. "I guess you could say—all that my life could be."

A smile grows on her face, and we walk toward the willow tree to join the others.

"Okay, so I want to hear the full story of the emerald." With her usual dramatic flair, Ashling leaves no doubt she's not taking no for an answer. "And don't leave anything out."

"Ah, a lover of tales. I'll tell ye the greatest tale in these parts, and it all begins with this ol' willow tree." Malachy is never happier than telling tales of long ago, and not so long ago, times.

Ashling settles in with anticipation.

Malachy begins. "This here willow tree was planted over three hundred years ago. A symbol of our family's strength and love over the years…"

As Malachy spins a tale of what could be considered epic proportions, I look at the people around me. Kayleigh on one side and Finn on the other. Seamus has claimed the other side of Kayleigh, and I've caught a few flirty exchanges.

While Malachy is finishing the tale with some embellishment, a garda pulls into the drive.

"Connell, what news do you bring?" Nora offers him a drink.

"Sorry to say, the bad kind."

"Oh, dear," Nora murmurs. She moves over a pace to grasp Malachy's hand.

"We've questioned Fiona extensively, and it looks like this goes deeper than we thought. Connections in Limerick are shady, and Ryan's nowhere to be found." He pauses a moment, then takes a deep breath and continues. "There's reason to believe this isn't over. A reliable source tells us Ryan is hidin' out, waitin' for the right moment to finish the job."

"What could they still be after?" I ask. "The emerald has already been found and turned in to the bank."

Garda Connell's mouth thins. "It seems there's a grudge that goes further back than the emerald. We don't know much yet, but we do know Ryan is not the leader. We believe it's comin' from the north."

"What kind of grudge?" Finn asks.

"The Irish kind," Garda Connell replies.

A tense silence follows as the news settles.

Malachy shakes his hand. "We thank you, Connell. Keep us updated."

We watch him walk away. Our joy has been dampened by the news as we wonder what will come from it all. What could cause a grudge so strong that people would kill for? And why the Kavanaghs and Brigid's Crossing?

Gandalf chooses that moment to jump the fence, a new talent of his, and trotted over to nuzzle Malachy at the willow tree.

"You will be the death of me," Malachy murmurs, but a smile spreads across his ruddy face.

"So this is the infamous Gandalf." Dad examines the horse to whom we owe our lives.

"'Tis. An ornery beast if ya've ever met one."

Gandalf whinnies in response.

"I think a trail ride is in order," Malachy declares, much to the pleasure of all.

As we saddle up the horses, each person is paired with a horse based on riding experience and personality. Every time I get into the saddle, I am amazed that these animals allow us to do so. What does that say about the horse? In my experience, most of them enjoy connecting with people, and it is, without doubt, a mutually beneficial relationship. At times, though, I wonder if we're not getting the better end of the deal.

"Hope we're not interruptin'."

Brianna and Shannon appear at the stable entrance, taking in our crew.

"Not at all!" Nora exclaims. "Come right in and meet the O'Reillys."

As my family greets the mother and daughter, I have the weirdest feeling of my two worlds colliding. But instead of crashing, they're blending into one.

"I won't be takin' no for an answer." Nora stubbornly hands Brianna a riding helmet.

"I've never been ridin' before." Brianna is hesitant.

"I'll stay with you," I tell her. "And you're riding Sam—he's the gentlest horse. You'll be safe with him."

Brianna looks at Shannon. "Well, if ya can do it, I suppose I can too."

Shannon lets out a squeal and Sam turns his ears toward the sound. He gracefully dips his head and nuzzles Shannon on the shoulder, causing the girl to laugh with uninhibited freedom.

Little miracles every day.

"Shannon and I are goin' ta have a grand time during your ride. Don't ya worry." Nora takes the girl's hand and leads her away to play with Ollie. The rugged sheepdog waves his tail in utter joy.

Excitement lends a little sizzle to the air as we mount our horses and lead them in a line toward the hills. Malachy is in the lead with Gandalf, the two of them completely in their glory. Both hold their heads high—proud and reliable, with a touch of the ornery.

"Can't believe I'm doin' this. I've always loved horses, but never brave enough to ride. I'm a coward," Brianna says.

"No, I'm sure that's not it. I think you're brave getting into the saddle today and even braver for letting your daughter ride. That takes a special kind of courage."

Brianna smiles at this. "Shannon's everythin' to me, and to see her so happy and improvin' with each ride…'tis a blessin'."

"The blessing of the animals."

At her questioning look, I explain. "It's a phrase my family always says. It's for those times when God blesses us through an animal. Research shows that the human-animal bond is responsible for a better quality of life for both the person and the animal. A strong bond influences our health and well-being. For instance, it lowers blood pressure and relieves stress, increasing the levels of dopamine. In a good relationship, there is security, comfort, and joy. It's the blessing of the animals."

Brianna smiles. "I love it."

"Finn and I hope that, when our program is up and running, we will be able to give more people the opportunity to experience it."

"A blessing indeed."

We ride in quiet for a while, taking in the natural beauty of the landscape. The ground is soggy, but the air is dry. The sun highlights the emerald green of the hills while a gentle breeze flows around us. This is perhaps the most beautiful day in Ireland yet.

As we turn back toward the farm, Aragorn's ears perk and he hesitates. I follow his gaze and spot two motorbikes on top of the hill. The hairs on my neck prickle as the two men stare in our direction. I stare right back at them, refusing to cower to my fear. After a moment they turn and drive off in the opposite direction, leaving the feeling that this fight isn't over yet.

~

I pack my bag later that evening, memories floating through my mind with each folded piece of clothing.

A soft knock sounds at my door.

"Come in."

Nora enters, carrying something in her hands. "I have somethin' for ya, dear." She hands me a brown paper package. I gently tear the paper away, revealing a freshly hewn St. Brigid's cross.

"Oh, Nora. How wonderful!"

"Well now, everyone should have their own cross."

"Thank you. I love it."

"And it will do nicely when ya two find your first home."

"True. Wait, what? Do you mean me and Finn?"

"It's clear as day yer made for each other."

I want to say that she's being ridiculous, but I can't argue—she's made a valid point.

"Nora, thank you for everything. For sponsoring us, supporting us, and caring for us like family. I can't wait to start our program and see where it leads."

"Ya are family. Ya and Finn were sent here for a reason. Don't ya ever forget that. I don't know how we would've been able to save the farm, if not for ya two. I'm just glad ya will be back in a couple weeks. Don't know what we'd do without ya 'round here."

She wraps me in a tight hug, and I let myself fall into her embrace. Even the peacefulness it invokes can't get rid of that nagging in the back of my mind.

"Nora," I whisper, "When we were out on the ride, I saw two men on motorbikes watching us. They saw me looking at them, then turned and rode away. But I think they were sending a message."

"Aye, I would say they were."

"Should we tell the garda?"

Nora considers this. "In time. I think for now we just need to have faith."

"So true."

"Did I ever tell ya the story of Malachy's cousin, James Brannan?"

I shake my head.

"That's a story of faith if there ever was one!"

"Well, you have to tell me now."

"James and his best mate, Michael, spent their childhood inseparable. Runnin' the streets and playin' football in a wee village in County Donegal. They grew up into fine young fellas and started fishin' together in the Donegal Bay. They were a sight to be seen. Brought in flounder, mackerel, pollack, codling, sea trout, dogfish by the bucketful. Natural fishermen they were. Wasn't a fish they couldn't catch."

"They sound like they were a great team."

"Aye. That they were. One day, Michael's sister joined 'em. Erin was a wee thing, not much older than ten or eleven with long, golden hair and bright blue eyes. As blue as the Connemara water, they say. She was the apple of Michael's eye, and a finer older brother there never was. Erin had been on the boat with them many times before, but that day a storm was brewin' off the coast."

Nora pauses and I lean closer, completely immersed in the story. "What happened?"

"The roughest storm in ages came upon the bay. Lightnin', hail, and tales of floodin' that left many a business ruined. People say it was like the end of times."

"Did their boat capsize?"

"Indeed. All three were knocked overboard, the waves makin' it nearly impossible to stay up. They were grand swimmers, all o' them, but were no match for the power of those waves. Knowin' they weren't to make it to the shore, they began prayin' for a miracle. That's when a piece of wood from the ship floated by them. James grabbed it and they were able to paddle toward shore."

"Oh, thank God!" I feel like I'm on the shore watching them in the roaring waters.

"Not over yet, dear. Just as they were closin' in on the shore, a rogue wave slammed into 'em—pulled poor Erin into the water and pushed the lads to the shore. The wave caused Michael to hit his head on the wood, and he was bleedin' in an awful way, in and out of consciousness. James ran back into the bay toward Erin's bobbin' head, but another wave crashed, and he could no longer see her."

"No!" The word escapes my lips before I can stop it.

"Aye, but James sent another prayer up to the heavens and by nothin' short of a miracle, the rain and wind stopped, and the sun's rays poked out from behind the clouds, shinin' on a spot of water. James dove under the water and pulled the lassie out. He swam all the way back to the shore on calm water."

"Did the storm really just stop like that?"

"That's what they say. No matter, it was his faith that saved Erin that day. And faith that led to the grandest friendship in all of Donegal. See, when Michael awoke and learned what James had done, he promised to repay him one day. And that day was just a couple years later when he bought an empty shop on Main Street, and they opened *O'Doherty and Brannan's Pot o' Gold*, the finest jewelry store in the county."

"They were partners?"

"Aye, a grand team."

"Wow. I would love to visit it one day."

Sadness clouds Nora's eyes. "Wish ya could. They sold the store years ago."

"Why would they do that?"

"Folks say there was a ragin' fight and the lads split ways."

"But they were so close."

"Aye," Nora says, with a faraway look. "Well, best be gettin' some sleep for your trip back to Maryland tomorrow."

"Goodnight, Nora," I whisper, giving her a hug.

"Goodnight, dear. Sweet dreams."

The night is full of dreams of Irish fishermen, storms, and pots of gold.

~

I walk through the front door of our old farmhouse, take in the family photos on the walls, and feel like those memories were a lifetime ago. In my bedroom for the first time in months, I walk around like I'm seeing my life for the first time. I have changed this summer.

I stop in front of the bulletin board hanging above my desk. To-do lists and schedules are scattered about—a web of stuff to hold me in place. Anxiety begins to tighten its grip around my chest, squeezing till I blow out a breath. I will not fall back into that trap. I pull each piece of paper down, one at a time, and watch as the cluttered mess reveals a blank board. I stare at it, thinking of the possibilities of an unplanned life. Pulling out a note from my bin, I write two words and then pin it to the center of the board.

To live.

That's a plan I'm ready to stick to.

Taking four more notes I write, *Second Chances. Family and Friends. Finn. School.* Those I pin them at each corner of the board.

Almost perfect. I pull one more note and write, *God*, and pin it to the top of the board.

Taking a step back, I examine the new reminders. Now it's perfect.

"I think we should have our own note—Sisters. The best combination of family and friends."

I turn to find Kayleigh and Ashleigh standing behind me, wearing amused expressions.

"I didn't hear you come in."

"We know. You were in the zone." Ashling scoops up the discarded schedules and to-dos. "Let's burn these. They deserve a fitting funeral."

Laughing, I pull my sisters into a hug.

"I can't promise to never write another to-do list or follow a schedule because, come on, they make good sense. But I can promise to not live by them."

"Sounds like your best plan yet," Kayleigh agrees.

My sisters do deserve their own category on my board.

"Girls, time to hang the cross." Mom smiles at us from the doorway.

"It was so nice of Nora to make us a cross too." Kayleigh takes the cross from Mom and studies it. "It's so beautiful."

"It really is," Mom agrees.

We hang it over the stable door, a physical reminder of God's presence on our farm and a nod to Finn's and my adventure. This cross has meaning to each of us now. I imagine St. Brigid sitting in a field, surrounded by sheep and horses, fastening the twigs to form the cross. Each fold and hook represent a special intention for the recipient and their home.

"It's awesome," Ashling says.

"A piece of Ireland right here at home."

"You'll have to tell us all about St. Brigid and Ireland," Kayleigh says. "Everything I've heard so far is fascinating."

"Right on. Anyone that can create a piece of art like that must be pretty cool."

"Something you both agree on. I can't wait to tell you everything."

I take in the moment, appreciating my family in a way I never did before. The next two weeks will be filled with family time and preparations for my freshman year. As much as I look forward to reuniting with Zoey and Kyle at university and beginning our program, I know the days at home will fly by. I want to savor every moment with my family before I leave.

We eat dinner out on the picnic table, a warm breeze flowing through the trees. Lightning bugs are taking flight, their golden beacons calling to one another. I breathe in the fresh air, filling my lungs before releasing it in a slow exhale.

"It's a sight that never loses its awe." My dad kisses my head before going inside. His chair slowly rocks to a stop.

My gaze returns to the field. The horses, majestic in their stride and purposeful in their speed, are living in the moment. How many of us can say the same thing? I know I have fallen short so many times. I make a promise to myself to be present in my days, to fully live in the moment, and to look for God in everything.

Pulling out my now-worn journal, I glance at the rapidly filling pages. Each one holds my hopes and dreams. It's a love story. One that began as a surprise, full of confusion and painful moments, but now it's the only thing that makes sense. As is true in most times of change, a mixture of sadness and excitement fills me. I uncap my pen and let my heart do the writing.

What an adventure this summer has been. I began this journey fully aware that this would be life-changing, but it was all for the wrong reasons. I thought it would be a platform for my education and career, and while that is still true, something even greater happened. My faith is renewed, and I see the value of living a life in service to others. How fulfilling it is to follow the right path. I am in love. Not the kind based on mere attraction and fun, but a deep, abiding love, one founded in faith and shared experiences.

I went to Ireland looking to find a place in science at the university, but what I found was my place in this world. I planned my life out to the last detail. Set everything up the way I wanted it to be, which was a good plan, but nothing compared to the plan God has for me. Only by giving up what I wanted, letting go of my own plan, was I able to travel the road He set out for me, a road that is so much more fulfilling than the one I imagined.

God has given me people to help me along the way, and for them I will be forever grateful. My heart swells thinking of Finn and our second chance at first love. We make the perfect team, picking each other up in our weaknesses and supporting each other in our strengths. The road ahead will not be easy, but I know God has amazing plans for our future.

Epilogue

One Year Later

"Ah, there's nothin' like being out on the water," Seamus tells Kayleigh.

We're all sitting beneath the old willow tree enjoying the picnic Nora prepared for us. Their heads are close, and there's a smile on Kayleigh's face that's never there when she's with Chris. I often wonder if they will break up now that they're attending different colleges. The look in Ashling's eye tells me she's thinking the same thing.

My sisters are visiting for a couple weeks as we're celebrating the end of our first year of college. University was everything I expected—long nights studying for exams, never-ending papers, quirky professors sparking curiosity in the most unexpected places, late-night roommate talks with Zoey…and then there's Finn.

"Your sisters are the best." Zoey laughs as Ashling acts out a scene from a recent school play. "Ashling is a hoot. And I see a little spark between Kayleigh and Seamus."

Kayleigh and Seamus walk toward the pasture, deep in conversation.

"Agreed on both," I whisper. "Kayleigh and Chris are still together, but you never know."

"You can say that again," Zoey murmurs, hurt still evident in her tone.

Zoey and Kyle's break-up after final exams surprised all of us. Neither of them is talking about it though. There's this tension in our group that's starting to feel like it's at snapping point.

"Any news from the garda?" Kyle looks awkward as Zoey sends him daggers.

"The past year has been quiet. Almost too quiet. The garda expect something's in the works but don't know what," Finn says. "They meet fairly regularly with the Kavanaghs, but there's nothing solid to go on yet—although they have started asking Seamus to meet with them too. Seems like something's pointing to Dublin Bay."

"His fishing team?"

Finn shrugs. "Looks like it, but we don't know for sure. Seamus seems to think that some kind of partnership formed when Ryan was working on the boat."

"I'm sure Seamus is keeping an eye out."

"He is. And with all of us, it's a hard match to complete with."

In Ireland, as the Kavanaghs taught us, you always fight for your family.

"Tommy and Antonella are a good team." Zoey nods in their direction, and I'm thankful for a change of subject.

Looking at the two of them, I can't help but agree. "They are complete opposites, and because of that, it just works in the arena. I'm so glad Antonella's staying in Ireland."

"You think she'll stay for good?"

"Hard to say. For now, it's where she wants to be. And she's wonderful with the children in the program. But I'm not sure how Tommy's dealing with it."

"Did he finally tell her how he feels?"

"Yup, and it wasn't what he hoped. She only wants to be friends."

They're grooming Bilbo, the Connemara pony with which Antonella and the children have found a special connection. Tommy watches her with an utter fascination that hasn't dimmed this past year. They both have found their places on the farm. Antonella gives Tommy direction, and Tommy provides support and care for her.

Zoey sends a considering look in Kyle's direction. "Maybe that's for the best."

I wish she would talk to me about this. I remind myself that I don't always have to do something or fix something. Sometimes just being there is enough. "Maybe it is." I put my arm around her.

She smiles and points to the sign by the arena. "There's always second chances, right?"

"Always."

Never has more truth been uttered in a single word. *Second Chances* has become a mantra for us around here. Our program has turned into a haven for not only those with special needs, but those who are looking for a second chance in life. Finn and I spend our weekends at the farm leading lessons and adjusting programs to fit the needs of the participants. Malachy and Nora are enlivened with the whole thing. It gives them new meaning in life, and they've taken to providing help whenever needed.

Finn and I have laid a strong research foundation centered on the positive effect of equine-assisted activities, especially therapeutic riding, in our research. The gains assessed in our trials have surpassed our original estimates, and the university agreed to help support our research for the upcoming years. After seeing firsthand what we're doing at Brigid's Crossing, they believe our research has the potential to lead a renewal in the field.

"Wanna take a walk?" Finn whispers to me.

"More than anything. Can you believe this time last year we were in the middle of an actual treasure hunt?"

He gives a little laugh. "A treasure hunt was the last thing I expected when I applied for the Emerald Isle program, but there were a lot of surprises last summer."

"I feel like we were always meant to find the emerald. Looking at it when the Kavanaghs untwisted that last bundle of twigs, it just felt, I don't even know how to say it. It was just *right*."

"That night, I knew something else to be true too. Every dream and hope I had for the future included one constant—you. You are in all my dreams and hopes for the future."

Before I can respond, he pulls out a ring, and I stop dead in my tracks, staring at a gold band holding a gleaming, heart-shaped emerald.

"This is a promise ring. I know we're young and we have so many dreams and goals. But I also know I want to be with you through it all. And I promise I will always be at your side."

"I love you, *mo anam cara*," I breathe.

"My soulmate," he murmurs.

I hold out my hand and he slides the ring on my finger.

"It's a perfect fit. Even looks like our emerald."

"It is our emerald." The twinkle in his eye is as adorable as ever. "Malachy had this cut out before turning the stone over to the bank. He said that whenever we look at it, it will remind us of our true treasure."

I look into the green gem twinkling on my finger and see our reflection there. Sometimes we all need a little Irish fairytale in our lives.

As for dreams, I'm in the middle of living mine.

Meet the Author

Colleen Marie grew up writing stories and dreaming of one day sharing them with the world. She is an MFA graduate in Creative Writing and a member of the Catholic Writer's Guild and American Christian Fiction Writers. Her stories inspire readers to see their unique beauty and intrinsic worth.

A great love of animals and teaching led her to a career as a life scientist and science educator. She founded Spirit of Love, an animal-assisted learning and wellness program promoting life-long learning and wellness through the human-animal bond. Animals weave their way into her tales, bringing a sense of the natural world with the fictional.

Colleen Marie lives in a small town in northern Maryland with her husband, three children, and crew of lovable animal friends. When she's not writing, you can find her teaching biology at a local university, enjoying family hikes through the woods, and traveling to find the most amazing homemade ice cream.

Visit her website at www.colleenmariewrites.com and follow along with her adventures on social media @colleenmariewrites.

Dear Reader

The Emerald Isle University Series is a New Adult book series weaving the stories of three sisters and their adventures of self-discovery and love in Ireland—the land of rolling green hills, mysterious legends, and hidden treasures.

The idea for The Emerald Isle University Series began after experiencing Ireland for the first time. It is a land of dreams and treasures, and the Emerald Isle made a lasting impression on my heart.

As the years went by, I found myself immersed in the field of life science and education while writing in those quiet moments. Then one day, I finally picked up the pencil and began outlining this trilogy. The series combines Irish culture and the beauty of the land with friendship, family, mystery, and second chance love.

I always hoped for a sister, so the idea of writing a series based on the connection between three sisters was a natural inclination. Each sister has her own unique story, but the bond of love and friendship between the three is unbreakable.

I hope you will join Teagan, Kayleigh, and Ashling on their adventures in the Emerald Isle and remember, there's a treasure waiting for each of us—we just need to take a leap of faith!

Next Book in the Series

Kayleigh's Knight
Emerald Isle University Series
Book #2

Coming 2025

Kayleigh O'Reilly has worked hard to have the perfect life. After graduating at the top of her class, her dream of becoming a writer is within reach when she's awarded a spot in the renowned Creative Writing Program at Emerald Isle University. Just as all her dreams are coming true, her world is turned upside down when her boyfriend breaks up with her the day she leaves for Ireland.

In the land of Saints and Scholars, Kayleigh begins her freshman year broken-hearted and in need of inspiration. Hope comes in the form of Seamus Murphy, the local fisherman and ruggedly handsome poet, and his offer to rent a small uninhibited cottage by the sea so she can focus on her writing. Feeling free for the first time, Kayleigh begins to rediscover herself and the dreams hidden deep in her heart.

Inspired by the enchanting town of Cloverdale, Kayleigh accepts a position at the local newspaper. The future is bright until she uncovers a deadly plot to revenge a decades old feud. Danger looms over the small town, and Kayleigh must decide who she can trust and if true love is worth the risk. As the storm threatens to destroy, will Kayleigh finally be able to find the words to write her own story?

Acknowledgements

I want to start by thanking you, the reader, for joining Teagan on her journey. I hope you enjoyed your time at Emerald Isle, and invite you to return and join her sisters in their stories. Kayleigh's story is coming soon!

Wishing heartfelt thanks to:

All of my early readers. Your feedback, reviews, and testimonials mean so much!

Michelle Buckman for helping with initial developmental editing and feedback.

Vinspire Publishing for giving *The Emerald Isle University Series* a home.

The many clients and participants I've worked with in equine-assisted activities. Your stories are the inspiration for this book.

My family and friends for your unceasing support. Especially, my parents for providing for me the experiences to allow my faith and love of animals to grow.

My children for always inspiring me and filling my heart with love each and every day.

And finally, I want to thank my husband, Bill, who always supports my dreams and helps me find time to allow those dreams to come to life. I love you and I am so grateful for this amazing life we have built.

Author's Note

I have always had a great love for animals and a fascination with the human-animal bond. This connection led to years of studying life science and researching the biological basis of that bond. My desire to learn as much as I could about it propelled me through many years of undergraduate and graduate work, earning a B.S. in Biology and an M.S. in Chemical Life Science. I studied tirelessly and spent over two decades working in animal hospitals, animal-assisted therapy organizations, and equine-assisted therapy farms.

It was on the farm that I felt the most at home. My connection with the horses made for a perfect fit as a horse leader in equine-assisted therapy and equine-facilitated learning sessions. I gave all in my studies and practical hours to earn my Equine Specialist in Mental Health and Learning (ESMHL) certification through PATH International.

In 2018, I took the leap and founded *Spirit of Love: Learning and Wellness LLC* as a way to bring together my love for animals, teaching, science research, and helping others. My hope was to bring animal-assisted interventions to more people in need. In the program I strive to nurture the human-animal bond by creating a relaxed and fun environment to encourage therapeutic interventions, promote a scientific basis for education within the field, and enhance the quality of life for those most in need. Teagan and Finn's program, *Second Chances*, was inspired by my work in equine-assisted therapy and the foundation my program, *Spirit of Love*.

To learn more, visit my program website at
http://www.spiritoflovewellness.com